Man of Two Tribes

ARTHUR W. UPFIELD

Man of
Two Tribes

ANGUS & ROBERTSON PUBLISHERS

ANGUS & ROBERTSON PUBLISHERS
London • Sydney • Melbourne • Singapore • Manila

First published 1956
This Arkon edition published 1981

Copyright Arthur Upfield 1956

ISBN 0 207 14102 9

Printed in Australia by Hedges & Bell Pty Ltd

Contents

Chapter One

NULLARBOR 'FRIENDS'

SENIOR CONSTABLE EASTER was roused by the alarm clock at three-forty-five a.m. He told his wife to sleep on, and passed to the kitchen where he fired the wood stove and filled the tin kettle, intending to boil water quickly.

He left the kitchen for the side veranda when the chill of the false dawn was dimming the stars, and there gazed eastward, seeking the first sign of the four-twenty express from Port Pirie. Beyond the house the world was without shape or substance.

Easter moved silently to the front veranda facing the railway buildings, the water tower, the oil containers for the new diesels, and the few cottages occupied by the permanent way men and staff. Other than all this, there was nothing of Chifley: no streets, no shops, no hotel. Save for one illumined window there was nothing of Chifley to be seen at four in the morning.

On a moonless night there is nothing to be seen of the Nullarbor Plain, or of the railway which crosses it for three hundred and thirty miles without an angle Euclid could detect, nothing of all those square miles of table-flat, treeless land beneath which the aborigines believe Ganba still lives and emerges at night to hunt for a blackfellow rash enough to leave his own camp fire to lure a wench from her lawful owner. Now were hidden all the caves, the caverns and blow-holes, and the miles on miles of foot-high saltbush searched by Senior Constable Easter and assistants for Myra Thomas, who disappeared from the four-twenty, five weeks and three days prior to this October morning.

Myra Thomas appeared to have walked off the train at one of the stopping places along the Transcontinental Railway, or had fallen from the train between stops, and in either case, old Ganba had gobbled her up for being out at night to snare another woman's lawful brute. Damn her, anyway!

Easter returned to his kitchen, brewed tea and set cups on the table without making one sound to disturb his wife. His face and neck and hands were the colour of weathered copper, his light-grey eyes a striking contrast. The sun and wind had bleached his hair and wrinkled his skin, making him look forty when he wasn't yet thirty. Such was his size and build that only a drunk would dare to start an argument.

His second cup of tea he took to the east veranda, and now light, neither false nor of the true dawn, arched above the edge of the world until it became a long blaze of white magnificence. The express was travelling this section at eighty miles an hour; and still fifteen minutes before it arrived at Chifley.

Well, he had done his utmost to find that blasted woman. Sixteen, eighteen hours a day had he toiled across the endless Plain, organised his trackers, who could find the imprints of a jerboa, but not the trace of a woman's foot, shod or naked. Week after week the search had proceeded without let-up, and never a scarf or a slipper had they found, let alone a body.

Yes, he had done his damnedest, and so had his trackers. His divisional inspector knew it, and had agreed that the fool woman must have disappeared intentionally.

Then why bother? Why search all over again, as though the woman was the wife of a Railways Commissioner, instead of being a murdering bitch who should have hanged

2

by the neck to stop her ever seeing the Nullarbor Plain? Well, he had better shine himself up to meet this top-notcher from the Eastern States who was coming to teach him, Senior Constable Easter, how to follow his forelock.

Shaved, and wearing drill tunic and slacks, Easter poured tea for his wife and swore at the train driver for hooting more than once at the long distance. His wife sat up, smiled her good morning, and asked him had he added coffee to the pot.

"Yes. What a slave I am! I put the grilling chops in the safe. Better go now to meet this bird."

"Sweet, you are. I'll get up now. Don't worry. We've had inspectors here before—hundreds of them."

Lightly kissing her hair, he moved to the door, looked back at her, and grinned because he didn't feel like smiling this morning.

She heard him pass along the short passage to the front door and down the veranda steps. The train was rumbling into what was called the station, there being no platform, when she slipped into a gown, added fuel to the fire and proceeded to dress. 'Just too bad,' was the thought in her mind. After all that work, all the upset routine. Now it would seem that bigger and better brains were to take over.

What did they think her husband was? A new chum? Hadn't he been born and reared at a homestead down on the south-west corner of the Plain? Hadn't he been stationed here for six years, and wouldn't take promotion because he loved every blessed mile of it? And why all the bother about such a woman?

It was all there in Elaine Easter's mind as she watched the coffee bubbling and heard the chops sizzling.

Toward the end of the previous August, Myra Thomas had faced the charge of murder. The trial was staged in

3

Adelaide, and in South Australia justice is rarely influenced by outside crack-pots.

She was twenty-seven, a smart dresser, and locally renowned as a radio script writer. The husband had been a radio actor, thirty-four years old, handsome, and, by all accounts, a perpetual drinker and an insatiable lover.

The Counsel for the Defence claimed that the husband had been the essence of a blackguard, and that the accused had long been a martyr to his mental frenzies and physical violence. The story went that the husband came home late from a 'conference'. There had been 'words' between them, and he had rushed out to the garage for a pistol. Subsequently there was a struggle, the gun went off, the husband fell dead. Same old story, proving that Australians are not original.

The Prosecution proved that the pistol, a war souvenir, had been recently oiled and yet required strong pressure on the trigger to fire it. The experts swore that the pistol was at least three feet from the victim's chest when discharged.

To the court officials and the press, the trial was just one of those things, but the accused provided much of interest to all men. She wept throughout. She wept during the judge's summing-up, and when the jury was absent. She wept whilst being escorted from the court by friends, to receive a mighty ovation from a crowd of teen-agers.

The jury's verdict was a mockery of reason. If ever the jury system was made to appear useless in murder cases, it was by this jury's verdict, tending to prove that, rather than accept responsibility for a hanging, it would acquit the accused.

For weeks prior to her trial, Myra Thomas received terrific publicity, which during the trial equalled that of the Melbourne Cup. But never a word was published in sympathy for the murdered man.

The 'heroine' and her mother decided to leave Adelaide

and live in Perth, W.A. They travelled under assumed names, and with them on the four-twenty express from Port Pirie were two other women. The beds were made up after the train left Reid. After leaving Fisher they all retired, and all slept fairly well, only one woman remembering the next morning that the train had stopped several times.

The conductor brought the morning tea when the train was between Deakin and Chifley, and then the three women discovered that the fourth wasn't with them. The train was searched without result. All stops between Chifley and Reid were contacted, but the missing woman had not left the train to be marooned. The train had to proceed, and the permanent way men searched the line, also without result. Finally, the weary Easter and his weary helpers gave up searching the country for ten miles either side of the line.

It had been hard on Elaine Easter, who had had to cook for and entertain inspectors and sergeants from both Adelaide and Perth, as there wasn't a hotel at Chifley. The poor things had to eat and sleep somewhere more comfortable than the engine sheds.

At last blessed peace and order, when the house was once again her own, as well as her husband. They could listen again to the sweet song of silence sung over the Plain at night, and now and then accompanied by the organ music of an approaching train. Books to read. Sewing to do. Recipes to try. The tucker-box to be packed when her husband had to leave on patrol. And now this! Another policeman coming even then from the standing train.

The diesel hooted and she heard the train pulling out on its long long way to Kalgoorlie in the west. And its music would dwindle and dwindle into the whispered lullaby of the Plain.

The aroma of coffee filled the kitchen, and the old American clock tick-tocking on the mantel over the stove had counted the moments for three generations. She placed the chops on a dish within the oven, and was surveying the breakfast table when she heard their footsteps on the veranda, along the passage. The train was sounding its nostalgic fare-you-wells, and the clock was striking the half-hour when they came into the kitchen.

The stranger was at first disappointing to Elaine Easter. She was accustomed to seeing very large men enter her kitchen, men with large square faces and small gimlet eyes which she always said they made small on purpose. This man was slight, wiry, dark-skinned, and the most amazing blue eyes she had ever seen regarded her as though appealing for forgiveness of the intrusion. She experienced a distinct shock when at the back of her mind she realised that he wasn't a full white man, but the shock was suppressed instantly by the charm of his smile as he waited to be presented.

Her husband put down the large suitcase, and she tried to avoid staring at him, because he was actually looking very happy. He said:

"Guess who, Elaine! Inspector Napoleon Bonaparte! He says we must call him 'Bony'. Says if we don't he'll recommend my demotion. Meet the wife . . . er, Bony."

Inspector Bonaparte! Her husband's tin god. The greatest crime investigator in all Australian history— according to her husband. The man who never yet had failed—again according to her husband.

Now she was being bowed to, and one part of her mind wondered why the other part told her that she was a woman, not just Elaine Easter. She was caught by the blue eyes and found herself listening with pleasure to his voice.

"All my friends call me 'Bony', Mrs. Easter. Even my Chief Commissioner, my wife and my sons, call me 'Bony'. I've been sure I would meet none but friends at Chifley."

Chapter Two

BONAPARTE'S ASSIGNMENT

AT breakfast the Easters were captivated by their official guest, but it was not until much later that day that they were able to analyse their reactions. Both were of what is loosely termed 'the bush', and they had expected their guest to be the opposite of what he proved to be—one of them.

That he was of mixed races they had to accept, reluctantly. His features and bearing were far removed from the castes with whom they were familiar along these southern districts of Australia, for Bonaparte had entered the world in the mid-north of Queensland, and his maternal ancestry had been powerfully influenced by the impact of the Polynesian peoples. When meeting the calm blue eyes and listening to the soft accentless voice, it was so easy to forget the duality of races.

Bony had crossed the Nullarbor many times, by train and plane; once only by car following the old telegraph route which skirts the southern edge of the Plain where it drops to the narrow coastal belt. Never previously had he been professionally interested in this part of Australia, and he anticipated no hardships additional to those he had experienced closer to the centre, such as the mulga forests, the gibber deserts, the desolation of the salt-pan basins. Although these several geophysical areas are strikingly different, common to all is the force of opposition to man, varied only by the circumstances confronting the individual.

"You have an office with the usual map of Australia pinned to the wall?" he asked, well knowing that the Police Station is the cross carried by every policeman in the true outback.

Easter conducted him to his own particular cross, where he lit the oil-lamp suspended from the ceiling, permitting Bony to survey the usual littered desk, the usual wire files hanging from nails driven into the walls, and usual large-scale map. Mechanically constructing what could be assumed to be a cigarette, he stood with Easter before the map on which someone had etched with blue pencil the area marked Nullarbor, meaning no trees. The cartographer had drawn a rule-straight line from east to west, and named this the Transcontinental Railway, the line bisecting the area.

"Authorities differ over the extent of this Plain," Bony said, without intention to teach but rather as a preface to what he had in mind to say. "It's probably much more than the estimate of thirty thousand square miles. What do you know of it?"

Easter's forefinger traversed the railway.

"Three hundred miles of dead straight line built on dead level ground, or what appears to the naked eye as dead level." The finger flashed downward on the map to within an inch of the coastline, moved slowly upward to cross the railway, continued upward until seemingly stopped by a blue dot named Lake Wyola. "From here down to the coast is something like three hundred miles. No trees, no surface water except in rock-holes filled by rain. Just a vacuum spanned by a railway, the railway stops by nothing but a few houses and servicing depots. No out-lying home-steads excepting to the south and one to the north-west. No roads but that coastal one. No fences, only land and the sky. That woman didn't fall from the train."

"Why do you think that?"

8

"I've a theory. No facts."

"Give me the theory."

"Well, I've always been interested in abnormal psychology," Easter said. "Didn't take much notice of the Thomas case because it was just another husband-wife brawl, but after the trial we dug up the papers and read the reports and got different ideas about the woman. When she disappeared, other things added up.

"I'd say Myra Thomas was vanity plus. She had tasted fame, strictly local though it was, but what a banquet during her trial! She finds herself hitting the headlines all over Australia. I'll bet no one received a bigger shock than she did when she was acquitted. What happened? She becomes the centre of nation-wide controversy, then within a week all the glory has faded, and the morons who screamed their admiration as she left court, deserted her to rush to the airfield to yell and scream their welcome to a foreign swooner. So, having dined with the gods, she must scramble under the table after the crumbs."

Bony was frankly astonished by this lucid exposition.

"What happens next?" proceeded Easter. "She planned the disappearance, planned it to take place in the middle of the fabulous Nullarbor Plain, the only place of its kind in the world and famous for just that. So she vanishes from a famous train when in the middle of a famous Plain. Sounds like poetry, doesn't it? Dressed in her night things and wearing slippers, she left the train at Cook and entered a car or truck driven by a pal who took her by the only track to the coast road, from which point they could go east or west into smoke.

"She certainly got what she wanted—more and more publicity which made the publicity at the trial look like a social paragraph. Now she will lie low for some time, and then reappear with the yarn that she had a sudden attack of amnesia brought on by the dreadful horror of the murder. Imagine the headlines! The money in the story of her life! That's my theory."

Easter found himself being studied.

"Were it not for evidence outside your knowledge," Bony said, "I would strongly incline to agreement. I want you to understand that I do agree that she did not fall from the train or wander away from it."

"I'm glad to hear that," Easter said. "I thought . . ."

"I know, Easter. Look at this map again. See here, to north-east of the Plain and far beyond its border, is the new town of Woomera, and away in the desert extends the rocket range. Now, much nearer, only a few miles north of Ooldea, along this east side of the plain, is the new atomic-testing ground called Maralinga. What blacks there were in that country have long since migrated to the southern extremity of their ancient tribal land, down near the coast, and so all the country of the range and testing ground is empty of native population. Now, north of this railway, as you pointed out, is merely a vacuum. We here at Chifley are almost at the western edge of the Plain, and the only station homestead within miles and miles is situated to the north-west of Chifley and called Mount Singular. Am I correct?"

"Yes."

"You know that Security at those Government establishments is very rigid. You don't know that Myra Thomas was a bad security risk during the war. D'you know a man named Patsy Lonergan?"

"Never seen him," replied Easter. "Heard of him. Once a prospector, now a dingo trapper, or was before he died at Norseman a fortnight ago."

"What do you know about him?" pressed Bony.

"Very little. Lonergan was trapping at Mount Singular for years, even before the present people took over the place, which is seventy miles north of the railway, and built on a bluff overlooking the Plain. He used camels, and like most old bushmen of his generation, he visited a township once every year for an extra good bender. Died when on that last one."

"Relatives of his live at Norseman," Bony supplemented. "When he died they naturally took possession of his personal effects, among which was his diary. Like many prospectors, Lonergan kept day-by-day notes of his catches, his lures and the condition of the ground feed and water-holes for his camels. His notes are cryptic, due to the old habit of the prospector giving nothing away so that should he turn up with a pound of gold, no one could back-track him by stealing his notes. Other than the current diary, no others were found, so we must assume that, as the notebooks were filled, he destroyed them. I'll fetch the diary from my suit-case."

Easter heard him talking to his wife in the kitchen, the tones of her voice conveying her easy acceptance of the visitor. He himself was feeling buoyant, for he had proof that his conduct of the search for the girl had been approved by the top brass. He was lighting his pipe when Bony returned with one of those long, ruled account books.

"From this diary," Bony began, "we know that Lonergan left Mount Singular on his last tour of a trap-line on July 6th, and that he returned to Mount Singular on September 4th. The girl vanished on the night of August 28th–29th. In camp on the night of August 26th he wrote: 'Camel feed pretty poor at Dead Oak Stump so came on to Nightmare Gutter. Got a half-bred pup at Dead Oak with Number Two. And two pure bred dogs at the 'roo I poisoned half a mile up the Gutter.' Those names mean anything to you, Easter?"

"Just a blank."

"The next day, August 27th, Lonergan wrote: 'Got to

Bumblefoot Hole pretty late. Water still plenty. Country much better this nearer to home. Picked up a quarter-bred at Bluebush Dip. Number Three Lure got her. Trap at Bumblefoot was sprung. Used Number Four in her. Number Four no good.' Bumblefoot Hole strike a chord?"

"Not a note," confessed Easter.

"Now the next day for Lonergan is August 28th," Bony continued. "At the end of this day, the entry was: 'Got to Big Claypan. Feed not too bad. Nothing in traps at Half-way Boozer. Brought the traps on and planted them for next trip. Weather been quiet and clear, but looks like rain tonight.' Still no chord?"

Easter shook his head, and Bony read the next entry:

" 'August 29th. Intended to camp at Lost Bell tonight, but was stuck up by a trap at the Three Saltbushes. Had to track the trap for more than a mile to where the biggest dog I ever got dragged it before he give it the works. No rain come. Feed hanging out pretty well here at Three Salt-bushes, but water in the soak dried up. Last night . . .' the vital night, remember, Easter, he spent at Big Clay-pan. . . . 'Last night around five in the morning was woke up by a helicopter. Could see the blades against the sky it was that low. Sort of proves my suspicion I heard a plane when I was camped at Bumblefoot a long time back.' "

"Helicopter!" breathed Easter. "Out there on that night of August 28th–29th, the night the woman disappeared."

"Where was the train at five o'clock that morning?" Bony asked.

"At Forrest being searched. Is that all about the heli-copter?"

"There is no later mention. Lonergan goes on to report that he trapped a dog at Curley's Hate, and found a trap sprung at Pigface Valley. How many helicopters loose in your district?"

"Not one. Some at the testing ground. They sent a machine over to join in the search for the girl. Stayed two days. That was a week after we began looking for her."

"They have two machines at Maralinga, and those machines were grounded from August 24th to September 6th, when one of them was despatched to hunt for the missing woman. When can we start for Mount Singular?"

"Mount Singular! Oh, any time. Inside an hour if you want."

"Make it inside three hours, Easter. I have to send telegrams to Adelaide."

"May I put a question?"

"Of course. As many as occur to you, Easter. Go ahead."

"You said that the Thomas woman was a bad security risk during the war. What's the connection?"

"She wrote the script for a radio show called 'Bless 'em All', primarily directed at the troops. It was before M.I., or whoever was supposed to look after subversive activities, realised that vital information could be passed to the enemy via our radio services. The show was a weekly broadcast, and she was abruptly taken off it.

"The main point is that Myra Thomas was once a security risk, and is still faintly regarded as such. When she disappeared within a few miles—comparative—of the atomic testing ground and the rocket range, the Security people in Canberra added the fact to their record. And then, Easter, when old Lonergan's diary turned up and a check was made proving there was not one registered helicopter within a million miles of their precious secrets, they actually added two to two, and came up with what certainly looks something like four."

"The relatives, then, sent the diary to Security?" surmised Easter.

13

"No. They handed the diary to the local police officer, who passed it on, and eventually it was received by your H.Q. in Perth. It was passed directly to Canberra, and at some conference or other it was realised that Longergan hadn't mentioned in his diary which direction the mysterious machine was flying when he saw it, and no one knew where such places as Curley's Hate and Bumblefoot Hole happened to be, as they were not marked on their maps.

"Fortunately, the police were represented at that conference by a firm friend of mine, Superintendent Bolt, who argued that one man on the ground would be more likely to succeed in locating the mysterious helicopter, the people flying it, their activities, and the association with them, if any, by the missing Myra Thomas, than could possibly be learned by a couple of fleets of jets flying around the Nullarbor Plain. When they asked him who the man on the ground was to be, Bolt had the obvious answer."

"You, of course," Easter smiled.

"Of course " Bony concurred without a smile. "Look! the day is dawning. The best time for meditation is when day dawns."

Meditation at daybreak; when the sun rose! Easter stood, scratched his chin, and docilely followed Bony to the veranda. He felt like the man who hopes to win a five-pound prize in a lottery and wins fifty thousand. He had searched for a woman at first thought to have fallen from a train; and now was given a picture of a female spy, mysterious helicopters, rockets and atom bombs.

Chapter Three

A SHIP AT SEA

THERE can be only one simile when telling of the Nullarbor Plain.

The jeep was like a ship on a completely calm ocean. To the east the sea was softly grey, and to the west it was softly green, and when the sun passed the meridian, the colours would be reversed. Astern of the jeep, three miles away, the tiny settlement of Chifley, despite reduction in size, appeared to be less than half a mile distant. The tiny houses guarded by the water-tower were the focal point of a fence built across the world. The wires could not be seen but the posts could be counted—telegraph posts flanking the ribbon of steel joining East with West Australia.

The track was merely twin marks of tyre-rasped earth and, between the marks and to either side, the foot-high salt-bush was the universal covering. Neither ahead nor astern could the motor track be seen beyond fifty yards, and one felt it was an eyesore and ought not to be there. The first exploring vehicle had to avoid rock-slabs and sometimes a rock-hole, and every succeeding vehicle had rigidly kept to those same tracks.

"This Mount Singular?" asked Bony. "Large holding?"

"According to the Survey not particularly large, a thousand square miles or so," replied Easter. "It's all open country, no boundary fences, and as there aren't any adjacent holdings, excepting to the south, the Weatherby cattle may graze over a million square miles of country, which varies a lot. Very few permanent waters. A salt-pan wilderness to the west, semi-desert to the north, this Plain to the East. I've never been farther north than the homestead, and that was back in 'forty-nine."

"The Weatherbys!" pressed Bony. "Old family? How many?"

"The first Weatherby took up the holding in 1900. By all accounts a hard doer who married a woman as tough as himself. Both died in the thirties and left the property to their two sons, Charles and Edgar. Edgar served up in the Islands during the war, and returned with his wife about the time I visited the homestead. They'd taken on a property in the west of New South which turned out no good, and the brothers decided to run in harness again. There's no white stockmen employed. Can't get whites these days. All the hands are aborigines."

"Where is their outlet point?"

"Rawlinna chiefly. Much farther for them than Chifley but better country to travel in wet seasons. Old Patsy Lonergan must have gone out that way, because he never caught the train at Chifley."

"Good citizens?"

"Never had the slightest trouble—officially."

An hour later the scenery was precisely the same, and Bony spoke again of the Weatherbys.

"As you said a while back, the Weatherbys seem to be good citizens, officially. Ever meet them socially, Easter?"

"Oh, yes. When they come to Chifley, which isn't often, they always spend an hour or two with the wife. Elaine likes the women very much although the wife of the younger brother, Edgar, seems a bit moody. The two men are all right, too. They mind their own business and don't pry into ours. Never any trouble with their abos."

"Eighty per cent of tribal strife has its origin in white

interference," Bony said, and then put another question:

"What communication have they with the outside?"

"Radio, that's all."

"Didn't they assist in the search for Myra Thomas?"

"Oh, yes. Spent about a week with my gang. Brought a couple of trackers to team with mine. And a side of the best beef we've ever lived on. You interested in them extra specially?"

"Only for the same reason that I am interested in the people living at other homesteads to the south and the south-west. If Patsy Lonergan wasn't mentally unstable due to his solitary life, if he didn't imagine he saw that helicopter, then that helicopter must have a base, and that base must be on or in the vicinity of the Nullarbor."

"Well, then, how do you propose to 'track' that machine? Search every homestead on the perimeter of the Plain?"

"No. Assuming that we found the helicopter at some homestead, we'd learn nothing excepting that the owner hadn't registered it with the Civil Aviation Department, and so had been breaking certain regulations. My interest is in the object and purpose for which it is being used on assumably secret missions, and merely locating the base won't satisfy me if the owner doesn't choose to talk."

"You're right there," Easter pondered. "What about my first question, about how you intend to 'track' that machine Lonergan says he saw?"

"I have letters from Lonergan's lawyer in Norseman, for the old fellow did own property and a sizable bank account for a prospector-dog-trapper. The letter empowers me, William Black, nephew of the deceased, to take over the camels, equipment and other things once owned by Loner-gan and now at Mount Singular. Included in those possessions are the dog traps, and it will be my job to locate them. To do that, I have to back-track the old chap along his trap-line, and locate his camps which he named so peculiarly. And then I have to hope . . . hope that I shall see or hear that helicopter, determine where it is going, and learn its business."

"Hell! What a job!"

"Easier, perhaps, than we think at the moment. So, I am William Black, the old man's nephew. You will recall that I visited you at your station this morning, as the Norseman policeman advised me, and it just so happened that you had to make the journey to Mount Singular for an official reason you have time to invent, and that you consented to have me accompany you."

Easter said: "I see," but Bony doubted it. They were silent during the next hour, at the end of which the scenery was exactly the same excepting that all that was left of Chifley was the water-tower looking like a black pebble lying on the horizon.

When Easter suggested lunch, Bony gathered dead brushwood and made a fire, and the policeman filled a billy-can and swung it from the apex of an iron triangle. The tuckerbox was unloaded, and while the water was coming to the boil they stood and surveyed the Nullarbor Plain simply because there was nothing else to look at.

"Must be unpleasant when a wind storm is working," Bony surmised, and Easter told of experiences when he had been glad to lie flat on his chest with a rock slab to anchor him to the ground.

"I understand there are no caves, caverns, blow-holes, north of the railway. Is that correct, d'you think?"

"None have been located," replied Easter. "But that means nothing to me because the country north of the railway hasn't been fully explored. It's all the same country, north or south of where they built the railway. There are other points, too."

"Such as?"

"It is said that the blow-holes are worked by ocean currents, that the sea tides force the air back into the galleries deep below and so create the underground wind. You know all that, of course."

"And that the noises underground have been attributed by the aborigines to the stomach rumblings and movements of Ganba the Man-eating Snake," Bony added.

"Just so. I've heard old Ganba roaring and rumbling below the surface and above it well down south of the railway. And I have heard him on the rampage well north of the railway, too. Even farther north than we are now.

"You've heard that even the station abos hate being out on the Nullarbor, I suppose," Easter went on. "Not only because of Ganba, but because there are wide areas where stock and horses won't pass over, and that spells underground cavities in the limestone, doesn't it? You really interested in caves and things?"

"No," admitted Bony. "I have inherited horror of darkness in a hole, yet I do not suffer from claustrophobia." He chuckled. "There it is, the fabulous Nullarbor Plain. All is visible, but what of those things that are under it? Up here we have space and sunlight and warmth. But no protection from the storms. Here there is nowhere to hide, no sanctuary, not even a tree to press your back against so that Ganba doesn't creep up on you. It would be decidedly unnatural for a man to enjoy such nakedness when standing on a bald world."

They ate cold roast beef and bread well buttered, and each was attacked by a thought neither would ever admit. The jeep was a good companion, was the little secret thought. When Easter stood beside it, the crown of his felt hat was the highest point within the completely unbroken, completely level horizon.

Not yet was Easter accustomed to the change which had taken place in the previously dapper Inspector Bonaparte. The smartly-cut grey suit had been changed for a worn drill shirt tucked into almost skin-tight trousers of grey gaberdine. The trousers were grubby in the right places denoting habitual contact with a horse, and although there were no spurs to the elastic-sided boots, their condition also hinted at much riding. Here in the broad sunlight his parentage was more obvious.

Bony sensed the scrutiny. Easter said:

"Have you decided how you will contact me after I leave you at Mount Singular?"

Bony looked shyly away from the big man. "I don't know, Mr. Easter," he drawled. Kicking a small stone, he regarded with apparent interest the jeep's tyres. "I'll be all right though." He laughed, superficially at nothing at all, gazed out over the Plain, anywhere but directly into the policeman's eyes. Continuing to kick at the stone, he repeated: "I'll be all right, though."

"By heck!" exploded Easter. "You've got the caste off to a T." Then suddenly serious, he added: "No offence meant."

"None taken, Easter. You know I once read a book about a very successful man who discovered that his mother was a quarter caste, and he so despaired that he hanged himself. How stupid! Why, he had every reason, in fact, to be proud of his success, like me. I am at the top of my chosen profession, Easter, despite all the handicaps of birth. Inspector Napoleon Bonaparte, Easter. With never a failure to his record. I never knew my father, and in any case it's a wise man who does, according to someone. I never knew my mother either. She was found dead under a sandalwood tree, with me on her breast and three days old. As you know, few go far in this country without the push of family, money, and social influence, but I have found my road in my own way, at my own pace, and no one tells me to do this or that."

"You have to admit, sir, that you're unusual," commented Easter.

"I know it. In spite of my parentage, I am unusual. Or is it because of my parentage?"

They packed the tucker-box and moved on under the midday sun. Later in the afternoon the horizon to the north-west to which they were travelling gradually humped into several blue-black pebbles, slowly to become rocks, to rise still higher from the sea to form the headlands of a coast when the Nullarbor was the bed of the Southern Ocean.

As the ship at sea, so did the jeep begin to skirt this coast, and soon they passed between two islands bearing trees, and a little later entered a wide inlet where the scrub on the high land either side came down to the beaches of narrow clay-pan belts. Abruptly the jeep turned into a beach and ran up between the scrub tree to undulating country.

"There is something I want you to do on your return to Chifley," Bony said. "Report the date you left me at Mount Singular. Add my last instruction to you, which is to make no attempt to contact me. Address the report to Box SS11, G.P.O., Adelaide. Clear?"

"Okay," Easter replied. "About a mile to go, that's all."

The track was now winding over the slight undulations bearing tussock grass, bluebush, currant and tea tree, and above all, the spaced bull-oak and the lesser belar. Cattle country, good cattle country.

Then the roof of a house appeared above the lower scrub, and eventually sheds and small dwellings.

The homestead was orderly, conspicuously tidy. About the main house of one storey and wide verandas was a white-painted picket fence, and when the jeep stopped before the main gate they could see the flower beds beyond and blooming rose bushes and water sprinklers which kept the creation alive.

In accordance with his role, Bony remained standing beside the jeep when Easter passed through the gateway to the front door. Before he could reach it, two women dressed in white appeared round the angle of the house to welcome him with obvious surprise and pleasure. What he said Bony could not overhear, but Easter also played the game right by not mentioning his passenger when invited to enter the house.

It was now about three-thirty, and Bony smoked two cigarettes and nothing happened. With the nonchalance of the aborigine, he loafed about the jeep and surveyed the place from the main house to the distant stock and horse yards. He could see a lubra taking washing from a line, and several aboriginal children playing under a distant oak. A little brown dog came to make friends with him, and a flock of black cockatoos came and departed with harsh caws.

Eventually, round the outside of the picket fence came an aborigine, walking with the effortless grace of the true wild man. Fully six feet in height, he was proof of good living. He wore an American-type wind-cheater, dungaree trousers tuckered into short leggings, and elastic-sided boots heavily spurred. A wide-brimmed felt hat completed the outfit.

Although fifty, he was clean-shaven. On both cheeks were cicatrices denoting manhood, and the hole in the septum through which is drawn the wand of the medicine man when in action told his rank. Over the wide face spread a smile not registered by the large black eyes. White teeth flashed when he said:

"Missus say for you come in for drink of tea."

"All right," Bony returned, looking shiftily at everything

bar those black eyes. "A drink of tea would go good."

Set beside Easter, D. I. Bonaparte was never insignificant. Set beside this fat aborigine, William Black felt himself a midget.

"You Kalgoorlie feller, eh?" probed the guide as they followed the fence.

"No. Diamantina." They were passing under a sugar gum, and Bony slipped off his shirt and undervest for the black eyes to feast on the cicatrices he bore on chest and back and upper arms.

"My father was brother to old Patsy Lonergan," he explained. "Patsy just died in Norseman. I come along for his camels and gear."

He prodded a forefinger into the fat covering the stockman's ribs, and they both laughed.

Chapter Four

JUST ANOTHER—HOMESTEAD

HAVING been served tea in a tin pannikin and cake by an immense aborigine woman in the men's meal hut, Bony returned to the jeep where he had to wait for Easter only a few minutes.

The policeman appeared with the women, and they came together along the iron-hard path made from pounded ants' nests to stand for a moment, exchanging final messages. At the time Bony didn't know that these two women were sisters, and there appeared nothing in common to lead anyone to assume the relationship. The elder was large and genial, her eyes being grey and her mouth generous. The other was smaller and slight, her dark hair closely cut. Her eyes were large and intent, and her smile was obviously forced.

Both in their early thirties, neither wore make-up, and the complexion of both was the work of the sun and the wind. The larger woman asked to be remembered to Mrs. Easter, and the younger then reminded him not to forget the mail, which was odd, because Easter carried the mailbag under an arm.

These women, especially the younger, reminded Bony of someone he had met, and he was working on the puzzle in a way one does when passing an idle moment, when Easter shook hands formally and emerged from the gate. The women turned back to the house, and Easter came to the jeep into which he stored the precious mailbag.

"I sowed the wheat," he said, softly. "The men are out but are expected back any time now. Told the women who you are, or are supposed to be, and your reason for coming."

"Good! Take it all right?"

"Oh yes. Said they thought someone would come some time about Lonergan's gear, or would write about it. I've got that job fixed in mind you want me to do. Anything else?"

"Having accepted an assignment, my superiors exhibit astonishing impatience for results, Easter. Probably within a week or two you will receive an enquiry concerning me. Treat them kindly, Easter. Say I said, 'Keep out and stay out.'"

"Or words to that effect." Easter grinned, knowing that he faced away from the house. Bony removed his swag from the jeep as Easter climbed in behind the wheel.

That was all. The policeman turned the vehicle and without even a wave of the hand, departed.

Standing loosely, Bony rolled a cigarette and lit it like the man to whom time means nothing. He was aware that he was under observation, not necessarily by the white women, for whom he would be of little interest, but certainly by the aborigines to whom he wasn't related, even to the fiftieth degree of tenth cousin, and had no possible totem ties. From now forward he must be William Black.

Having tossed his swag into a scrub tree, safe from the assault of the homestead dogs when they returned from work, he walked the fifty odd yards to sit on a boulder overlooking the Nullarbor Plain. It was then four o'clock.

At ease, he gazed outward over the Plain, four hundred feet below. To the south and north were other dark headlands of this inland coast. Before him was space and sunlight to quicken a man's imagination, and behind lay the

tree shadows, the rolling land and the dunes of white sand
to give a sense of security and illusion of his own im-
portance, providing comfort after the chill of nakedness
imposed by the Plain.

No wonder the aborigines didn't like leaving this coast to
venture far out on the sea of saltbush. They would want
wood for real fires, not brush which makes a passing flash of
heat. They would need something material back of them o'
nights so that the Spirit of this land they named Ganba
would not steal upon them and breathe cold air between
their naked shoulders. Man made only one careless slip in
this country; by instinct the aborigines were never careless,
and there are white men, but rare, who never make a slip
and never are caught by Ganba.

Old Patsy Lonergan was one of these. He would leave
this homestead with two camels and a dog, vanish within
Easter's vacuum, and reappear after weeks to 'put in' his
dingo scalps and be credited with the bonus. He would
repeat this, perhaps three times a year, and on the money
enjoy a genuine bender lasting a fortnight or three weeks.

A foolish man? Of course not! There has to be a balance.
If the body is starved it must be saved from death by food.
And if the mind is pounded by threats of Ganba, then
alcohol is an antidote, to balance the ledger of life, for
alcohol is the open sesame to social conviviality so essential
for the maintenance of sanity in the victim of solitude.

It was a pity that his current diary was begun only in the
previous January, and that it covered merely the last
expedition and that preceding it. Otherwise there might
have been further reference to the aircraft he had heard
when last at the camp he named Big Claypan.

He was a bright boy, that real nephew at Norseman who
had located the diary. He had nous enough to understand
the implication of the old man's note on the helicopter. His

report on the mental state of his uncle, added to that of the local policeman, removed doubt that Lonergan had imagined he had seen it. Aircraft at night over that part of Ganba's country could have had no legitimate cause, its destination not a homestead, decidedly not a town or city, for none of these are within the vacuum.

The explosion that diary triggered! The messages and signals, the conferences! Spies sneaking around the back fence to watch atomic tests! As though the spies would be silly enough to leave Canberra where they gain all they want in cosy bars and at official cocktail parties.

Nonetheless, there was official as distinct from police interest; official interest being entirely confined to the preservation of what is called Security; police interest concerned merely with what had become of a missing person. And the two interests connected only by a sentence in a dingo trapper's diary.

A day or two at this homestead might provide a lead from the aborigines. Little escapes their observation. The head stockman had become friendly once he had seen proof of the stranger's sealing into the unknown tribe in faraway Queensland. Bony had given nothing of value beyond the 'fact' of his relationship to Lonergan, and the purpose of his visit as well as the reason for being so far south of his Queensland tribe. And he had been given nothing of value excepting that the dingoes were not as numerous as some years and that they seemed to be keeping to the areas verging on the Plain.

Lonergan had owned two camels and a dog named Lucy. His gear and personal effects were still within the hut he always occupied when at the homestead and which he kept locked during his absences. His traps the head stockman knew little about and, with a chuckle quite divorced from humour, he told Bony that if he wanted to locate the traps he'd have to go out and find them. Where? In what direction? Another chuckle. A wave of the hand like a compass needle twitching from a flea bite.

No mention of a helicopter. But then no mention of the windmills, of the station utilities, of the Melbourne Cup about to be run. Black had asked no questions, not even where he might find his uncle's traps. Like the ordinary aborigine, William Black metaphorically pulled his forelock to the medicine man.

He watched Easter's jeep when it left the 'coast' and went to sea, a tiny boat with an outboard engine, producing a short wake of thin dust. Finally all Black could see of it was the tiny dust puff which soon floated away. Seventy miles to Chifley! Just steer and wait for Chifley to come to you.

When the sun was casting its shadows far out upon the Plain, a slight noise caused Bony to turn and see the large man who was approaching him from the house. He walked with the unmistakable gait of the horseman, and was dressed in the unmistakable fashion of the cattleman, the faint tinkle of his spurs having been the sound to attract William Black.

"Good day-ee! You Black?"

Bony stood and with slow and bashful drawl replied that he was.

"I'm told you are Patsy's nephew. That right?"

Black essayed a smile of assent, kicked the dust with a boot, and from a shirt pocket produced the letter from the Norseman lawyer. He was a handsome man, this Weatherby, burned dark by the sun, made strong by the fight to succeed, poised like the man accustomed to giving orders. His dark eyes keenly examined the face of the lesser man, and his mind subconsciously noted the scuffing of the boot, the nervous reaction when in the presence of a superior. Accepting the letter, he broke the envelope and read it slowly as one habitually averse to scanning anything, be it a steer or a letter.

"All right, Black, you can collect your uncle's stuff. We don't want it, of course." The voice was clear and deep, the accent ingrained by the 'old' school. "All Patsy's things are stored in a hut we let him use. There's a credit on the books, too. What about that?"

William Black hesitated, and Mr. Weatherby snapped fingers.

"Well?"

"Better let it stay, Mr. Weatherby. The lawyer never said nothing about any money. I can tell him."

"All right! Tell him. You had better come to the office for the key to the hut. And before you go, you must make out a list of the things you take. Write?"

"Yes, Mr. Weatherby."

The cattleman moved away, and Black took his swag from the tree and slouched after him to the store building behind the main house. The office was merely a corner of this store, stocked with foodstuffs, machinery parts, drapery, and a hundred other items needed on such a place.

"Now don't forget that list, Black," Weatherby said. "I'll have it made in duplicate and you can sign one and I'll sign the other for the lawyer. In the morning I'll have the boys bring in the camels. The old man pass out comfortably?"

No hint of sympathy. Barely of interest. A hard man this Weatherby who, Bony surmised, was the elder of the brothers.

Again William Black sniggered, looked at everything save the man at the desk.

"Drunk as Chloe, Mr. Weatherby."

The next question Weatherby put was wholly in order as the subject was the always problematic financial state of a gold prospector. He asked if Patsy Lonergan had left much of an estate, and was neatly informed that the lawyer hadn't read the will excepting to a daughter and another nephew.

"H'm! What part d'you come from?" was the question bound to be asked by any intelligent white man, and this one was satisfied with the answer, and didn't smile when William Black told him that Lonergan had spent several years in Queensland when a much younger man. The dinner triangle was beaten and Weatherby rose from behind the desk, saying:

"Your uncle was a tough old timer. You know, Black, now I come to think on him, he wasn't so silly as he made out sometimes. The country got him all right, there's no doubt about that. It'll get any man who goes into it alone for weeks and months, and the man who does go out alone prospecting for metals and scalps and suchlike may be a fool, but he's a damn courageous fool. Now you go along to the men's quarters for dinner. See you in the morning."

"Thanks, Mr. Weatherby," William Black said respectfully, and departed.

Already in the meal hut were several aborigines, including the head stockman, and two half-castes. The head stockman laughed at him, but pointed to the huge aborigine cook, saying:

"See her, Bill! She's the cook aroun' here. Good cook, too, but jus' nag and nag."

There was a general guffaw, and William Black smiled at the lubra, having met her at afternoon smoko. She served him with a great heap of roast beef and vegetables, and laughingly told him to return for more. Indeed a happy race that employs laughter to hide many things, which includes nervousness with strangers.

They wanted to know where he came from, so he explained where the Diamantina country is, and how he came to travel down to Norseman, and how he was related to Patsy Lonergan. They were genuinely sorry to hear that Patsy had died, and laughed delightedly when he told them that Patsy passed on when 'as drunk as Chloe'. And Bony knew that this friendly reaction to him was based on the opinion held by the medicine man-cum-head stockman, but they did not accept him as one of themselves and would not have been friendly to the stranger had he intended to seek work with them, or attempt to join their conservative community.

Following dinner, one of them pointed out Lonergan's hut, then all of them wandered away to the scrub behind the homestead where doubtless their humpies would be.

The hut contained but the one room. There was a rough bunk fashioned with poles, to which was stretched hessian bags and bearing on them a hessian mattress stuffed with straw. The late tenant had stowed his camel gear in here and Bony had to carry the pack-saddle and the riding-saddle outside before he could move about. Until it was almost dark he proceeded with the inventory, noting a pair of well-kept leather saddle-bags, a pair of five-gallon water drums, hobbles and noselines, a tucker-box, blankets, old clothes, including an overcoat with silk lapels which must once have been worn by a duke when waiting on Queen Victoria.

He was lighting a hurricane lantern when a sound at the door brought to notice the wriggling body of a small brown dog of United Nations breed, small bright eyes, and ears which one ancestor had influenced to droop.

"Who are you?" asked William Black, and the dog entered and jumped to the bunk where she settled and coyly told him she was Lucy.

Chapter Five

MILLIE AND CURLEY

EARLY the next morning the horse tailer brought in Lonergan's camels. Actually they were the descendants of the originally imported dromedaries of one hump, but like most words requiring slight effort to pronounce, the shorter and inaccurate designation was ever employed in Australia.

Millie and Curley were in fine condition, and Bony found them in a high-railed yard, placidly chewing cud, and in their eyes the expression of resignation to more ruddy work. Millie was lighter in colour than her boy friend, and both appeared docile. Millie had her nose-plug in position, but Curley wore a strong leather halter, the ragged hole in his nose telling a story.

"Had experience with camels, I suppose," remarked Weatherby, who had approached with his brother to join Bony at the rails. The younger man was slighter than the other, even darker of hair and eyes, and he lacked the outward placidity of his brother.

"Yes," admitted Bony, and returned his gaze to the camels.

"They're quiet enough, but a little tricky. Made the inventory of your uncle's gear?"

"Most of it, I reckon. There's still the traps. The old feller didn't bring them in."

This was met with a silence attributable perhaps to the

interest the others had in the camels. Ultimately the younger Weatherby said:

"As no one knows where old Patsy set his traps, you'll have to pass them up."

"Looks like it," agreed the older man. "I doubt that the abos even know which way the old boy put down his last trap line. Be out west because that's where the dogs are this year. Hey! Ringer! Come here."

The head stockman, who was leading a saddled mare from a yard, led her to his employer. He was looking hard and efficient this morning.

"Any idea where old Patsy worked his last trap line?" Weatherby asked, and Ringer smiled and kicked dust.

"Dunno," he replied. "Ole Patsy cunnin' feller all right. Tommy seen camel tracks other side of the Splinter . . . jus' before the rain. Could be, old Patsy worked them salt-pans out there."

"All right, Ringer. You get going, and don't forget to look-see at Mason's Hole."

"Those traps hardly worth going after, even if you knew where to look," remarked the younger Weatherby while rolling a cigarette. Casually Bony turned to him, his face empty of expression as they expected. This younger Weatherby seemed to be stronger in character than the other, and about him was an aura hinting at a far different background. Although dressed for riding and with that horsey appearance common to all cattlemen, he lacked the ease of movement.

"Better find 'em all the same," persisted William Black. "The lawyer said I had to bring in everything belonging to my uncle."

"Not worth the trouble and time," stressed the younger man. "Still, if you want it that way . . ." Sliding off the rails, he walked away to the house, his body upright, his legs straight. The elder Weatherby said:

"Old Patsy pottered about this country for years. Where he set his traps no one bothered to ask. If you must go looking for traps, Black, just to satisfy a lawyer, then you'd better make for the Splinter and pick up the camel tracks from there—if you can, because it rained seventy points since Tommy was out there."

"Where's this Splinter, Mr. Weatherby?"

"You take the Rawlinna track out by the blacks' camp for about three miles. At the three-mile there's a branch track out to a bore, six miles on. There's no track beyond the bore, but keep on for another twelve miles when you'll come to an upthrust of rock we call the Splinter. No water except in shallow rock-holes. You'll have to take what you can and go easy on what you take. Claypan water is too salt for men, but the camels can exist on it." Weatherby slid to the ground. "Anyway, complete that inventory and we'll fix it before you leave. You take my tip and forget the traps."

Bony remained on the rails like a man confronted by a problem. Lucy came and slipped under the bottom rail and pranced daintily about the camels in the yard, passing between their large flat pads with the familiarity of established comradeship.

The request for the inventory of Lonergan's property was reasonable. There wasn't much to it, and it was not intended to include the contents of a small and battered suitcase found under the bunk.

The willingness to have the camels yarded was also reasonable, as was the recitation of the difficulties surrounding the location of the dead man's traps. The attitude to him, William Black, of the Weatherbys was normal. The entire atmosphere of this homestead was normal, too.

There was, however, one oddity. The previous day the

head stockman said that the wild dogs were working north of the homestead. This morning the head stockman had supported Weatherby's contention that the dogs were working over the salt-pan country to the west.

Returning to the old trapper's hut, Bony completed the inventory and checked the tinned foodstuffs and other items Lonergan had left within the saddle-bags and the tucker-box. Then, taking the stout calico ration bags, he crossed to the rear of the house to purchase what he needed.

An aborigine maid told him to go to the store where Mrs. Weatherby would serve him, and he had waited minutes when the younger woman appeared and led him inside. The questing eyes gazed upon him without interest, and her expression gave him the feeling that she never really smiled.

"Now what is it you want?" she asked sharply, and so began the business of buying flour, sugar, tea, tinned meats and jam, salt and sauces, tobacco in plugs and cigarette papers and matches.

"P'raps Mr. Weatherby would set the bill against what's owed to my uncle," suggested William Black, and the woman nodded agreement and pushed forward the docket for him to sign. "I've fixed up the list, too."

"Then I'll make it out in duplicate. Wait."

She typed with professional speed whilst Bony leaned against a stack of cases and wondered if he had actually seen her before coming to Mount Singular. Her husband, the younger Weatherby, intruded into his mind and rang a tiny bell which produced no answer to its demand. The machine spilled the papers and the carbon, and Mrs. Weatherby dipped a pen into ink and proffered it, saying:

"You write very well, Black."

That was a slip, a small slip, in the building of the character of an itinerant half-caste, a faint flaw in otherwise perfect work, and he experienced annoyance added to that occasioned by the failure of the bell.

"Liked writing at school," he said. "Not much good at anything else." He signed both typed sheets, and regained his hand-written list. "Mr. Weatherby'll sign, too," he said. "The lawyer . . ."

"Don't bother with them, Black." Her large eyes were mere pools of brown and expressed nothing, and Bony wondered at the utter lack of entity. "I'll have Mr. Weatherby sign right now, and you can take a copy before you leave. All lawyers are fussy persons, and you needn't take much notice of what they say."

He managed a shame-faced smile at his own stubbornness, thanked her in a casual manner and carried the rations back to the hut, where he proceeded to set out the gear ready for packing on the camels. Lucy ran to meet him on his arrival at the yards.

The noseline, a light line to which a loop of twine was attached, was expertly tossed over Millie's head which was drawn down to slip the twine loop about her nose-plug. She wanted then to chew Bony's right ear, but there was no viciousness. The free end of the noseline was dropped to the ground while Curley was being attended to, and, to Bony's amusement, the dog daintily took hold of the line and led Millie to the yard gate.

Curley had to be dealt with differently. He held his great head high, and his eyes flashed with sudden rebellion as Bony approached him. As a youngster he had been cruelly treated, when the plug through the nostril had been torn out in his effort to avoid blows to his head. Like the cat, the camel can never be wholly conquered, and like the elephant, its memory is everlasting.

Bony managed to grip the end of the short rope dangling from the halter, and he pulled on this to bring the beast's head low enough to couple the halter line. The dog, leaving Millie at the gate, came and barked at Bony, and he dropped the line, which Lucy gripped by her teeth and, docilely, Curley followed her to join Millie.

She couldn't lead both camels at the same time, and so Bony took them to the hut where he 'hooshed' Millie to her knees beside the riding saddle she was to carry. She didn't go down with any sign of happiness. In fact, she was playing a game and any intelligent student of camel psychology could follow it.

Now and then she pretended to make the attempt to rise. The saddle was lifted over her hump, and she pretended that it hurt. She moaned protests as the saddle was being strapped under her chest and down under her snake-like neck. One would think she was being subjected to gross indignity, and the act was put on solely for Curley's benefit. Curley was the bad boy who had to be roused so that when his turn came he would be in a tantrum and perform to anger this biped who was putting her to work. Horses cannot think like that. Beside the camel, the horse is brainless.

As planned, Curley was ready for the fray when his turn came. He pranced and bellowed when the halter line was hauled down and he was ordered to 'hoosh'. He fell on one knee, and up again, to kneel on the other. He roared and danced; and Millie looked on, and her eyes plainly said to Bony: 'How are you liking that?'

Bony unhurriedly took up a loading rope and tossed one end behind Curley's legs, and Curley knew that to rebel any longer would mean being tied down. So, without being ordered, he fell to his knees, grunted, and settled himself beside his pack-saddle. The game was over, and Millie sneered her contempt. A lion! Baa! Just another lamb.

The pack load most be accurately balanced. To each side

of the straw-stuffed pack were hooked the saddle-bags and water-drums. On top were piled the spare rations, the swag, and the tent, the load then being roped. Through the rope was thrust the axe, and, to counter-balance the weight, the dozen iron tent pegs and telescopic pole. The riding saddle of iron was furnished with a bag cushion to sit behind the hump, and in the fore-part was strapped the tucker-box carrying food and eating utensils in current use. Another bag containing a fry-pan and billy-cans was fastened to this saddle and balanced by the rifle slung from the opposite side.

All this took a little time. The gear was in fairly good condition, but the rifle was a jewel, and had been the pride of old Lonergan's heart. A Savage, point 25, a high-powered weapon, it was kept and carried in a soft leather case.

"Seems that you know how to work these brutes," remarked the elder Weatherby, who had approached from Bony's rear. "Here's your signed copy of the inventory. Still determined to look for the old feller's traps?"

Nodding, Bony gazed at his feet, then glanced up and past the big man's eyes.

"Have to give it a burl, Mr. Weatherby. Make a try just to say I did. I take the track out past the blacks' camp for three miles, then leave the track and follow one going on due west to hit the bore. That right?"

"That's right. And twelve miles on from the bore to hit the Splinter. There's no permanent water beyond the bore."

"I'll give it a burl, anyhow."

"If you must."

Careful to the last, Bony kicked at the dust, gazed about the homestead as though sad at leaving it, essayed a shy smile, and said:

"Reckon I'll give a day out from the bore lookin' for them traps, and then I'll make south down to Rawlinna."

"Good idea. Waste of time looking for them, Black."

Bony urged the camels to their feet. He tied the end of Curley's halter line to the riding-saddle, took up Millie's noseline and proceeded to lead the string of two away from the homestead, out by the motor shed, past the men's quarters, which appeared wholly unoccupied, and then skirted the aborigines' camp, comprising bag humpies, lean-tos and smoking camp-fires about which squatted men, women and children, silent, watchful and interested in the departing strange man from the Diamantina.

Ten minutes later Bony was still walking, the nose-line hung from the crook of an arm. Millie was resignedly chewing cud. Curley continued to moan. Lucy ran on ahead, constantly looking back.

And so began the search for Lonergan's last trap-line, that camp he named Big Claypan, from which he had seen the unknown helicopter, the search for a dust mote in a vacuum.

Chapter Six

LONERGAN'S PALS

IT is not pleasant to know you are being followed. Foot-steps behind, that alter their rhythm when you do, have a peculiarly sinister import, especially when the night is dark and street lighting inadequate. Bony could not hear foot-steps behind his short camel train, for the winding track was soft underfoot, but his suspicion was born of expectancy, and steadily nurtured by the birds.

The track was like a snake's trail, meandering through clumps of gimlet trees, skirting an occasional rock knob, crossing shallow depressions bearing thick waitabit and jamwoods.

When they had travelled more than a mile, Lucy ran off into the scrub and waited for them to follow her lead.

Neither pausing nor calling to her, Bony continued right ahead, and at once Millie began to tug gently against the noseline and softly moan objection to going forward. Curley was even more reluctant. He bellowed and walked sidewise, pranced and tucked his hind quarters under his load, hopeful of it becoming unbalanced and falling from him.

Careful not to betray any curiosity in that turn off, Bony determinedly continued along the track, compelled by Curley's behaviour to glance constantly backward, and at the same time seeking for a hint of an unknown follower.

There are two causes for camel rebellion: leaving the

home paddock, and travelling over country not recently visited, if at all. Like the dog, they wanted to take that turn-off—merely a pad now washed out by the rain—because that was the way old Lonergan had previously taken them. To the northward, not to this westward country of salt-pans.

Outwardly the camels were resigned when the track branched, the main branch continuing away to the south. Bony followed the lesser track which would take him to the bore, six miles farther on, and decided to continue walking as he would have better command over the camels who, although now docile, still had fire in their eyes.

Now and then he stopped to test the ropes on Curley's pack, pretending nervousness of the balance of the load, the while he listened to the birds whose persistent warning of the presence of someone back along the track convinced him that the follower's job was to be certain that he did head for the bore.

Why this interest? The head stockman had said the dogs were working to the north of the homestead, then, in support of the Weatherbys, that the dogs were numerous to the westward. And, further, that an aborigine had seen the tracks of Lonergan's camels westward of a rock upthrust, called the Splinter.

Why this effort to prevent him, William Black, from going northward? It was to the north of the homestead that Lonergan had his trap-line. Lucy and the camels plainly said so. Gold! Was gold behind the conspiracy to get William Black out of this country and back to Rawlinna? Old Patsy could have been on to gold. He could have mentioned his 'find' to the Weatherbys, although it was most unlikely he would divulge the locality. Or were they, despite the normalcy of their homestead, associated with that mysterious helicopter?

They had never mentioned to Easter that Lonergan had

seen this helicopter. A tit-bit of bush news, it was most likely he had spoken of it, and for reasons of their own they had decided to let the subject die with the old man, unaware of the diary he kept.

Anyway, he, William Black, was being seen off the premises. That was now certain, because although some birds are arrant liars in matters concerning their own affairs, they never lie to each other concerning the activities of bipeds, and quadrupeds like dogs and foxes.

The birds told Bony that the follower gave up when about three miles from the bore, but there remained the necessity of leaving proof on the track that he and the camels actually did reach the bore, and proceed beyond it. And so, all the way the camels left proof on the sandy top-soil.

It was past two o'clock when he reached the bore of the non-flowing type, necessitating a pump and windmill to work it. It was not pretty country, being semi-arid, drab in colouring, the scrub stunted and almost useless for stock. There was water in the line of troughing, but no wild dogs had visted this place since the rain of a week or two back, and none of their tracks were on the road from the homestead.

After a meal and an hour's rest for the camels, Bony led them directly to the west. There was now no road and the farther he proceeded the poorer became the country. Despite the recent rain, there was no surface water.

Six miles beyond the bore, Bony decided to camp for the night at the edge of a depression, and unloaded the animals amid the low scrub and took them to the saltbush where he hobbled and belled them.

As customary, they stood facing each other and conversed with their eyes, clearly exchanging views about this new master, this ugly country which might spring nasty surprises on them, and the general cussedness of life. Lucy squatted beside Bony's fire and watched them and, when the conference was over, both camels pretended contentment until they thought the man had forgotten them, whereupon both abruptly headed eastward for the homestead paddock, making for low scrub where they could be detected only by the dwindling sound of the bells.

A loaded camel will walk all day at two miles and a half to the hour. A hobbled camel will travel one mile in an hour when controlled by the insatiable urge to return to some place or other. Here is a land where distance is measured by the hour, where only the initiated can hope to move from one point to another, and where only the bush masters can find water. There were no landmarks, just dun-coloured scrub with an occasional green-black tree growing a little taller. There were no rabbits, and, Bony was convinced, the dogs and foxes had deserted a long time since.

Before sundown, Bony went after the camels and brought them to camp, where he tied them to stout scrub trees for the night. The slight westerly wind dropped, and only the occasional clank of a bell disturbed the complete silence. This land was deserted, even by the birds.

They left camp the next morning before sunrise, both camels still resentful. In case anyone at the homestead might determine to track William Black as far as his first night camp, Bony led the animals directly to the south-east and towards far distant Rawlinna, thus registering his decision to abandon search for the traps and to return to Norseman. Two miles he proceeded on this course before again turning to the west, and following another mile, turned to the north to begin a giant curve which would bring him to the Nullarbor Plain some twenty miles to the north of the Mount Singular homestead.

Long distances, many miles and many hours, to thwart a trailer.

Immediately they headed northward the camels became Little Lord Fauntleroys, although they were hungry and had no cud. Lucy expressed her happiness by trotting ahead. The sun shone warmly, the flies were less irritating, and thus all was well. Bony was able to ride, and Millie walked with a swing like a girl taking pleasure in swirling her skirt to best advantage. Curley swung along behind her, head high, eyes bright, hungry and no longer rebellious.

Toward four o'clock they reached open grassy spaces, and narrow belts of wattles in late golden bloom, and a few minutes later Lucy sat down abruptly and smiled up at Bony. She sat on a narrow camel pad which the rain hadn't entirely obliterated, and here Millie evinced desire to follow this pad to the homestead. He had to dismount to compel her to follow him to the north, and half an hour later, he sighted five sandalwood trees beyond which was nothing but the sky.

These five magnificent trees appeared to be guarded by great boulders, and amid these boulders Bony found evidence of a camelman's camp.

The place was on the point of a promontory overlooking the Nullarbor. Here were the everlasting daisies, flannel bush, luscious waitabit and other delectable feed for camels, and Bony could not unload and hobble fast enough for Millie and Curley.

This was Sandalwood Camp, mentioned in the diary and the second camp out from the homestead. In a natural haven provided by three boulders was a heap of ashes proving the heat of many fires lit by lonely old Patsy Lonergan, and it was here that the character of the man first emerged for Bony.

He left it to the very end of the day before bringing the camels to neck-rope each to a tree. They were tired, replete, placid, prepared to camp for the night, and when it was dark he could see their pale shapes, and they could see him squatted about his fire as he kneaded baking-powder dough and finally placed it in a bed of hot ashes. It was then that first Curley and then Millie became restless, getting to their feet, lying down, rising again, and continuing thus to register growing emotion.

The ants could not be the cause. Hunger was certainly absent. They had been broken in to going without water for three days, so thirst wasn't worrying them.

While the bread was baking, Bony opened a tin of meat for himself and the dog. He had placed the tucker-box to gain the firelight, and before the box had laid out Lonergan's tablecloth, a yard square of canvas. Lucy now crouched close by watching him, and when offered the meat in the opened tin, she wrinkled her nose and looked offended.

Bony ate, and she continued to regard him with pleading eyes, until he thought he knew what troubled her. The meat had to be cut and served on a tin plate. She ate daintily, then asked for a crust of the bread loaf, and he was astonished when she carried it at once to Curley.

Curley's moaning ceased. The dog returned to beg for another crust, and this she took to Millie. Thereafter, both animals laid themselves down and seldom moved until day broke.

So there was a facet of a dead man's character. His dog had to eat from a plate, and his camels had to receive a crust of bread taken to them every night by the dog. Doubtless the old man would converse with his three animals. Assuredly it would be a one-way traffic, opinions and questions and answers all verbally expressed, but not necessarily a one-way traffic of thought.

These three animals were now at a place they knew, and now they demanded the attention which was customary at this place. The previous night, out in the salt-pan country, the dog hadn't asked for a plate, and the camels hadn't demanded bread crusts.

Having washed the limited utensils, Bony poked the ashes with a stick and raked out the now perfectly baked loaf. He could hear faintly the gurgle of cud when brought up the long neck to the throat. The stars were lamps, indeed. At a distance a fox barked, and on a branch of a sandalwood a mopoke 'porked'.

As man has ever done, Bony squatted over the tiny fire, now and then pushing the burning ends of wood into the central glow. It is a time for cogitating, a time for mental relaxation into which often intrude vital thoughts and pictures. Questions were under the surface of his mind, and at odd moments these had stirred throughout the day.

Why had the attempt been made to 'slew' him away from this north country bordering the Nullarbor Plain? To all intents and purposes it was a no-man's country. Uranium instead of gold might be the answer. But, were it a question of gold or uranium, why the necessity of employing an unregistered helicopter?

Was there a helicopter? Had imagination dictated Lonergan's note on the helicopter by sheer coincidence with the night the woman vanished? It resolved to fact or imagination: it must be reduced to the minimum by establishing the state of Lonergan's mind.

The reports he had seen on Lonergan, written by the dead man's relatives, the Norseman policeman and the hotel-keeper, contributed to but one picture. Lonergan was old but still physically tough. After long abstemiousness once he broke himself in, he could out-drink men half his age and, no matter his condition, could speak intelligibly. The Norseman policeman had stated that Lonergan's mental condition was that of an old man who had lived too long in solitude, that his mind wandered when asked questions, and that this wasn't intended evasion.

This to Bony was the crux. The diary proved deliberate evasion of the facts of his travels, although this could well be the habit of many years. Still, there must be taken into account the manifestations of solitude, because solitude does produce extraordinary results, many of which the professional psychologist would decline to consider. These Bony had to contend with when taking his first step toward the authenticity or otherwise of that entry.

The next day was greeted by the camels and the dog with that absence of irritation ruling when routine is being followed. Millie sank to her knees without objection, to permit Bony to mount behind her hump. Curley gazed amiably about the night camp and decided to behave. Lucy regarded man and animals, and then actually led the way from camp—to the north. The family was harmoniously complete. The sun rose in the usual place, and the sky was cloudless.

For an hour they proceeded along this verdant strip overlooking the Plain, and then Lucy led down the slope to a blunt inlet, from which they moved on to the Plain and continued northward.

Bony now had to rely entirely on the dog and the camels to take him from camp to camp, made previously by Patsy Lonergan.

Lonergan had written: "Nothing in trap at She-Oak Rock."

They came to a great rock which appeared as though it had tried to roll on a tree. The tree was a she-oak, and at the foot of the tree was a trap holding a golden dog fox. Lucy sniffed at the carcase, then lifted a lip at the rider. Again, as William Black who might still be followed, Bony slid down from the high saddle and removed the scalp, which was worth at this time, two pounds. The trap he hung in the tree.

Without bothering to settle Millie in order to mount, Bony hauled himself up to the saddle, and they went on. He did nothing to drive or guide. The animal followed the dog, and sometimes the dog followed Curley, and the way hugged this 'coast' of steep slopes with its promontories, bays and inlets and little islands off 'shore'.

At one point Millie turned into the cliff and halted at the foot of a landslide years old. This puzzled Bony because there was no mention in the diary of such a place for a trap. He prospected on foot, and found that the rubble contained quartz, and that Lonergan had stopped here to nap some of it for possible gold content. The camels hadn't forgotten that for them it had been a temporary rest camp.

The same thing happened towards sundown. Both camels stopped on a shallow shelf of white sand footing what appeared as a dangerous rock overhang. Bony wasn't impressed by the site for a camp, but Curley went down to his knees and yawned, and Millie looked round at her rider and followed suit when Bony delayed ordering her to 'hoosta'. He would have gone on, but both camels said plainly with their eyes 'This is where we camped last time. So what?'

Having been unloaded and hobbled on good feed, the camels held conference as usual, and, when agreement had been reached, they turned southward and shuffled away.

"If you don't settle down," Bony called after them, "we shall go on until dark."

They didn't even look back. Curley did pause now and then to snatch a mouthful of fodder, but Millie went on steadily until she had a lead of a couple of hundred yards. Then Curley realised he was being left behind, and he bellowed and lunged with hobbled feet to catch up with her.

Eventually they disappeared into the mouth of a gully,

and because they might reach the upland Bony went after them with the noseline and the halter.

He found them in what was actually a narrow cleft bordered by sheer rock faces. They were facing about, waiting for him with obvious impatience. Then he found the rock-hole covered with rough timber and weighted with rock slabs to prevent wild animals falling in and polluting the water below. It meant a trip back to the camp for the bucket.

Eventually, the camels went to ground and spent a half-hour chewing water-moistened cud, while Bony sipped hot tea and watched the cliff shadows racing away across the Plain. Soon it was dark, and the bells tinkled contentedly that the camels were feeding not more than a hundred yards away. Then the bells rang a different tune, telling that the animals were coming hurriedly to camp, and into the light of the fire appeared their heads on a level as they waited for Bony to cut a crust for the waiting dog to serve to them.

And thus was Bony taken to old Patsy Lonergan's camps, with no roads to follow, no tracks to lead him. To Lost Bell Camp. To another named in the diary as Menzies's Delight, although what this bare, unprotected place had to delight Mr. Menzies, Bony could not name. He was taken to the Three Saltbushes camp, where a dingo had dragged a trap away for more than a mile; next day on to Big Claypan which was out of sight of the 'coast', and where old Lonergan had noted in his diary that he had seen the helicopter.

Having timed the hours of travel, and multiplied the total by the average walking pace of the camels, Bony estimated that he was now ninety miles north of Mount Singular.

Chapter Seven

BEWARE OF GANBA

ON all this grey and purple world, seemingly completely flat and visually round, there was nothing higher than Bony's head. All day man and animals had moved across this sea of saltbush, never higher than Curley's knee and, because of the absence of objects, only by gazing directly downward on the bush did Bony retain the sense of movement.

Shortly after five o'clock, when all the bush to the west was purple, and that to the east was silver, there appeared ahead a thin dark line, which slowly thickened and eventually widened to disclose a circular depression having a diameter of half a mile, the level floor being some twelve feet below the Plain.

Bony guessed this to be Bumblefoot Hole, and subsequent investigation proved Lonergan's naming of it when he found the long dead remains of a dingo which had been trapped and had gained freedom. The bones of its left fore-leg proved the point, for the extremity was a mere drumstick.

Following days and nights of utter defencelessness on the Plain, Bumblefoot Hole was the ideal camp, appreciated even more by the camels than their master. Lucy piloted the way down the steep cliff-like edge, and later Bony found that this was the only way down or up for the camels. On the floor of the depression, the feed was good, and the diary had mentioned that here was another water supply.

To the right of where they reached the floor were the rain-washed ashes of Lonergan's fires, and in the face of the cliff nearby were several small caves, one of which was filled with dry brushwood obviously stored by the old trapper.

After the animals had led him to the rock-hole water, and he had set his tea billy against the flames of a fire, Bony explored the caves. There were three on this arc of the circle, and in one he found a ten-gallon oil drum one end of which had been cut away to provide the rock lid, and another that had been used for water storage.

In the first he found tobacco and matches in air-tight tins, tinned meat and fish, boxes of cartridges for the Savage rifle, bottles of strychnine, pain-killer and liver pills, leather for straps and hide for hobbles and thin rope for nose-lines.

Quite a camp! Proving? Proving that Lonergan's last trap-line had not been temporary, supported by his well protected water-holes.

Bumblefoot Hole was certainly a hole, a place to hide in, safety from that Something from which nothing could be concealed, not even the thoughts running through a man's mind. To arrive here was not unlike entering a house that is warm and quiet after the door has been slammed against the storm. Once here, a man begins to feel the effect of that bald empty world spinning in space. He remembers how he looked back over a shoulder, subconsciously shrinking from the Something that was tracking him, stalking him, watching, waiting. He recalls an old fable the abos tell about Ganba, and right now he isn't in the mood to lift his lip in a sneer at the ignorant, benighted blackfellow.

Were he a new chum who happened to stumble into this hole, he would stay and, having eaten old Lonergan's reserve store, starve and die in it because he would be too damn frightened to leave it. Old Patsy was hardened against Ganba. He had grown a shell about himself. His bald world did have companions—two camels and a dog—with whom he could talk, over whom he could exert authority and so retain something of a sense of values. Doubtless he heard Voices, and spoke to them in return, but he wasn't that mentally off balance as to relax his defence against the Plain.

Old Lonergan had neither exaggerated nor had been inaccurate in anything jotted into his diary, from this Hole right back to Mount Singular; therefore, Bony's opinion firmed still more that the note concerning the helicopter was based on fact. Although the old man had not mentioned the direction of the aircraft, if taken in conjunction with the disappearance of the woman, it was reasonable to assume it was flying north.

What lay to the north? Only more and more Nullarbor Plain, a wide area of claypan and water-gutter, then the ground rising from the Plain to the Great Inland Desert, so-called, which extends almost to the coast of North Australia.

Next day Bony remained at Bumblefoot Hole. He washed clothes and troubled to cook something resembling an Irish stew. Once he went up the camel pad to the lip of the cliff with the rifle, hoping to see a kangaroo, their fresh tracks having been seen by him in the Hole. He spent two hours with the old diaries and papers within the battered suitcase he had found under Lonergan's bunk in the homestead hut, but these gave nothing but proof that the trapper had established other trap-lines.

For Bony this day had a Sunday atmosphere, for most bushmen wash clothes on Sunday morning, and read the racing journals during the afternoon. When the sun retired, he went again to hunt for kangaroos, and to his satisfaction

saw four does, two sizable joeys, and two young bucks all
feeding some two hundred yards distant.

Already the light was failing. There was no wind. The
surface of the Plain appeared to be sinking into a fast-
deepening green, and the sky into a fast-brightening dome
of matt ivory. Having settled himself, Bony whistled shrilly
to bring the 'roos to upright attention.

The report was followed by no echoes, being just one
mighty whip-crack, and, placing the rifle carefully beside a
boulder, Bony walked from the Hole to the carcass of the
young buck.

He removed the skin and left the fore-quarters, and then,
when beginning the return to Bumblefoot Hole, discovered
that it had vanished into the now universally black surface of
the Plain.

He found himself walking in a vast chamber having no
walls, and a ceiling of arching blue. The chamber was
padded not only to stop sound from getting out, but to
prevent it from getting in. Sound was a mirage for the ears,
and silence was real and menacing, pressing against the ears
so that the heart could be heard working like the engine
it is.

On reaching the lip of the Hole, he paused to welcome
the red star of his camp fire and the relief to his ears brought
by the sound of the hobble chains affixed to the camels' feet.
The recent impressions were still influencing him when the
ghost of a sound stopped his foot from beginning the
descent.

It wasn't caused by the dog, for she was lying beside the
fire. The sound appeared to originate from one of the stars
pointing the Southern Cross. It was moving now to the
Three Sisters, just a whispered threat . . . oo-a-i . . .ar-r-
a-i . . . oo-oo . . . ish-ah. The sound grew. It came over
the edge of the now invisible world. It sped towards

Bumblefoot Hole and the man standing at its verge. Abruptly it halted, then veered to the north and ran away under the ground where it 'hoomped' and 'grumphed'. Up it came to race about the Plain with gathering speed, to draw close, to halt. Where? You couldn't tell. Then it whispered, and the whisper grew to become a rumble which rolled fast towards Bony, finally to sigh with infinite glee right at his back.

The hobble chains continued to clink musically, and the dog continued to lie sleeping by the fire. Turning about, Bony bowed to the Nullarbor Plain, saying:

"Greetings, Ganba! Some other time. Good night!"

(Imagination! This is a report, not a fantasy.)

The night was kind, and Bony slept until the hobble chains told of the camels getting up for breakfast. He ate grilled 'roo chops and he grilled meat for Lucy, and as the sun was firing the horizon he led the camels up from the Hole.

He urged Millie to her knees, and when mounted merely relaxed in the saddle and waited. Lucy ran a little way to the southward, and he shook his head and called; then she ran to the northward and Millie turned to follow her.

When the sun said it was a few minutes after eleven, Lucy raised the first rabbit Bony had seen since leaving the station homestead. The dog's chance was Buckley's. Millie turned her ears back towards her rider, turned them front again and minded her own business for ten minutes, then stopped and asked a question. Curley strained to walk on to the right, where could be seen a ribbon of blue-bush growing in a wide gutter.

This was Bluebush Dip mentioned in the diary, and proved when Bony found the place where the trap had been set, and the carcass of the dog whose capture also was recorded in the diary.

As the camels insisted that this was a rest camp, Bony brewed tea and ate lunch of tinned fish and bread.

Early afternoon, the camels evinced slight nervousness, appearing to place their big feet with caution. The ground was littered with limestone chips, and here and there bare rock created naked patches on the saltbush covering. The way twisted a great deal although the overall direction continued to the north. They took two hours to pass over this wide area of subterranean caverns and passages and blow-holes. And at five o'clock they came to Nightmare Gutter.

Nightmare Gutter was a zig-zagging crack twenty feet wide and some ten feet deep, an obvious barrier to the traveller northward bound, for old Lonergan had with the shovel cut a road down and up the far side. Here he had camped, and here Bony camped.

The next night, camp was at Dead Oak Stump, and, as noted in the diary, the camel feed was poor. Dead Oak Stump! The name indicated a tree, and there wasn't a tree for hundreds of miles. He found the carcass of the half-grown dog Lonergan had recorded, but not for some time did he locate the stump.

It was less than eighteen inches high and told of a tree, old when it died, a tree that must have lived before William One upset the Saxons. The stump was so dry-rotted that Bony could have knocked it out with the axe, and refrained, thinking that this old stump must have had sentimental value for Patsy Lonergan.

A man mentally unbalanced is incapable of sentiment. That stump would make a snug fire on a cold night, where all the fuel was brushwood, which burned barely long enough to boil water. Old Lonergan probably loved this Plain, every mile of it, although each mile was exactly like every other mile. He came to this place at long intervals, and would, as Bony now did, stand and gaze at a tree stump because it was rare and therefore precious. It had been his stump, as this was his camp, like the other camps he had made and called his own. Likely enough he greeted it, farewelled it, remembered it often and wondered how it fared during his absence.

And thus Bony's faith in the dead man's mental integrity was strengthened.

Time by the stars was eleven-thirty, and he had been asleep for two hours when he dreamed he heard Ganba and woke to hear Lucy muttering in alarm. Sitting up in his blankets beside the now dead fire, he detected the far-off noise of an engine, coming to them from the south-west. The sound was not the rhythmical tune of an aeroplane flying at great height, and in volume it increased but slowly. Eventually it passed to the north-east, and several miles eastward of Bony's camp and, although Bony knew little of aircraft engines, he was sure that this machine was not an aeroplane.

He heard it again shortly before three o'clock, returning on the same course.

When day broke he was ready for it, but he gave the camels another hour to feed. He was feeling gleeful, as any man would whose hunch was being proved by fact. Before the sun rose to blur distance with its colour-loaded brush, he could see a red-brown stain above the northern horizon; and beyond the edge of the world that way, perhaps thirty or forty miles, was the limit of the Nullarbor Plain, for that red mark was sand, the sand of the Central Desert which, following a great rain, will bloom like Eden. And at some pin-point on that vast map the aircraft had touched down, remained a little while, then taken off to return to base. That pin-point had to be found.

A change had taken place in this man of two races, a

change begun by the angry threat of Ganba when at Bumblefoot Hole, and carried forward by the sound of that aircraft. Ever the inherited influences of the two races warred for the soul of Napoleon Bonaparte, and it was the very continuity of this warfare which had created Detective Inspector Bonaparte, and which time and again prevented him from sinking back into the more primitive of the two races. When Constable Easter and his wife met him he was suave, outwardly arrogant, inwardly humble, conscious, and justifiably so, of his long succession of triumphs, not only over criminals but over that half of himself he feared. Now the Easters might not have recognised him.

When at Mount Singular, he had acted the character of the half-caste to perfection. Now he acted, without conscious effort, the character of the full-blood aborigine, for his maternal instincts were in the ascendant.

Today his eyes were never still. From his face was gone the usual expression of calm confidence. He glanced constantly to the rear, jerking his head when normally he would have made the movement with deliberation. The Plain was at long last making itself felt, as it had made itself wholly felt on the full bloods, to the extent that they would not spend a night on it. It could be that the change in this man was being transmitted to Millie.

Today she walked on her toes. Today her cat ears constantly turned to the rear, and constantly she looked to the right and to the left.

Chapter Eight

BARRIERS OF STRAW

THE Plain was a tessellated pavement, hurrying black shadows coming to meet the camels and giving the rider the impression that he was travelling at high speed. The sky this morning was uniform cadmium between isolated clouds, and the wind from the northern desert was warm and scented, yet filled with the promise of heat and dust.

About mid-morning Bony sighted an abnormal feature which proved to be an apparently endless ribbon of straw about twenty feet wide, and in places a foot thick. It lay approximately east-west, and from the condition of the straw, he thought it must be at least a year old.

Reference in the diary to the Buckbush Road had aroused his interest and, now that he gazed upon it, he was reminded of the Yellow Brick Road to The Wizard of Oz. A mile or two farther on was another buckbush road, and the next day, yet a third ribbon which was much less weathered, and which gave the answer to the riddle.

There was a year of wonderful life and vigour in what is stupidly called the 'Dead Heart of Australia', when the alleged desert bloomed with an extraordinary profusion of flowers, and when all the earth was vivid green with buckbush.

This annual shrub will grow to the size of a water ball, and when dead is a sphere of filigree straw. The wind snaps it from the parent stalk and rolls it onward. Millions of these balls, driven by the wind, will roll over the ground like hurdling horses, will pile against fences until the barrier is such that the following balls 'run' up and over.

At the end of this fertile year, the north wind had driven the buckbush from the desert uplands down to the Plain, and the saltbush had opposed it until it had gathered into a rope many feet high and many feet thick, when the entire rope of miles in length had rolled on and on. Then, when the wild wind had dropped, the ropes of straw became stationary, and the rain had come to sodden and rot them.

Old Lonergan had named one of his camps The Brisbane Line, the term being a sarcastic reference to an imagined plan of defence when the Japanese were doing their stuff. It was the fourth camp north of Bumblefoot Hole, and on the southern edge of a straw barrier which Bony estimated as being twelve feet high. As far as he could see to east and west, there was no break save that at the camp, which had been made by the old trapper with the smashing blade of a shovel. And there it would remain until another mighty wind moved it on again.

Beyond this wall of straw the going was again dangerous, being littered with rock chips; areas of rock roofing beneath which were caverns and passages. Bony saw holes, some having a diameter of a few inches, others of several feet. Many holes were easily seen, others were masked by salt-bush, but Millie knew the track and never once faltered or evinced fear. All day they had travelled over this dangerous country, and Bony hoped to camp at what Lonergan called The Belfry. The horizon, still distant, was now broken by what seemed to be ridges of red rock, but were the summits of sand dunes.

There was certainly nothing between him and those sand dunes indicative of a church, and when the sun was sinking under the Plain his attention was drawn to a swirling column of dark 'smoke' issuing from the ground as though from volcanic action.

The camels had no fear of this place: Millie hastened her pace to reach it. The 'smoke' endlessly whirled upward to be flattened as though by a cold wedge when less than a hundred feet above ground, and Bony could detect the units comprising a great host of bats. They came up from a small replica of Bumblefoot Hole, and so entranced by them was he that he was almost thrown out of the saddle when Millie 'flomped' to her knees, yawned, and told him to get on with the job of making camp.

There, but a few feet beyond her head, was the site of Lonergan's camp fires.

The bank of the hole nearest the camp shelved slightly to the cliff-face, and from this face the bats continued to issue, in number not to be estimated. Obviously they inhabited an underground cavern, which Bony had no intention of exploring. He found Lonergan's water hole and, having watered the camels, he lit a fire and watched the emergence of the bat army.

Night was chasing Day beyond land's end, and the bat cloud banished the glory of the evening sky as Bony shovelled earth over his fire, laid out his bedding, and drew the unpitched tent over himself and the dog, who liked bats even less than he. There would be no bread baking this night, and when Millie and Curley came close for their usual crusts, to find the cupboard bare, they put themselves down beside the tent covering and sulkily went to sleep.

Their bells roused Bony at dawning. Then the sky was clear and the stars were bright, but with the daylight came the bats from all quarters, to hover again like a rain cloud which formed a living water-spout gradually descending into the cavern. Before the sun rose there wasn't a bat above ground.

The days passed and the camps were left behind:
Lunatic's Moan, a blow-hole from which air rushed with
a continuous moaning noise; Lover's Lane, where was a
rock-hole between two great barriers of straw. Since
Lonergan was last here, both barriers had been moved and
the trapper's path wiped out but Millie ploughed through
the masses, a ton of which would dwarf a cathedral.

It rained half an inch the night they spent at Curley's
Hate, and the next day they walked up from the Plain on to
the wind-ribbed sand of the desert, then turned east to reach
the extremity of Lonergan's trap-line, where they found his
fire-site in the shadow of two belar trees. Trees! O blessed
trees! To hear the soft sunset-wind singing its lullaby in a
roof of trees! Far into the night Bony sat by his fire of solid
wood, and frequently praised old dead Patsy for having
named this place The Bushman's Home.

The rain had filled the shallow claypans between the
dunes, and water had run into the deeper depressions along
the verge of the Nullarbor Plain. On the lower dunes the
young buckbush attracted the camels, but even so soon
after the rain the wind crested the high dunes with red
feathers.

The rain provided independence of rock-holes, but it
was also disadvantageous in that it wiped smooth this page
of the Book of the Bush, and thus much valuable information would be withheld until time enabled the new
printing to be done.

Bony remained in camp at The Bushman's Home for two
days, scouting on foot, when he chanced on a group of
kangaroos, and bagged one. Wild dogs were here, and
rabbits were numerous, and all this world was kind and
protective.

But inland from this northern 'coast' the country rapidly
deteriorated. Penetrating it for three miles, he found that

the dunes dwindled into a sea of spinifex slopes and naked gibber flats, the gibber stones so polished by the wind-driven sand particles that the upper surfaces reflected the sun with such power as to torture the eyes. Far to the north lay a line of flat-topped residuals, red and bare, and onward for two thousand miles it would be just the same as this picture of the Great Inland Desert, populated by aborigines never in contact with the white man, and so dispersed that for one to be killed by a rocket would almost be an impossibility.

Bony wondered who the heck would want to open this back door to Australia's atomic secrets.

From this point he travelled along the verge of the Plain where the going was easy, making to the east to 'cut' the line of flight of the aircraft he had heard when at Dead Oak Stump. Fortunately the surface water held. Kangaroos were numerous, and the rabbits promised the summer, if it behaved, to make of themselves a plague. Bony passed colonies of jerboa rats; the roofs of the 'houses' well secured from the wind with stones. Bell birds mocked from the scrub trees, and at night wedges of ducks lanced across the sky. The crows were busy too, and altogether Bony found these days most pleasant.

When the camels first became restless, he attributed it to their normal dislike of unfamiliar country, there being nothing else to account for it. The country was open. The weather remained perfect. He found no tracks of wild aborigines nor any other indication of their proximity. Lucy was neither restless nor suspicious, and normally a man can place full reliance on a dog to inform him of anything unusual.

On being confident that he had actually 'cut' the aircraft's line of flight, he camped under a most ancient box tree growing on the edge of the Plain. This night he pondered on his next move, squatting beside his fire, and, as men of all nomadic races have done, he drew with a pointed stick a map on the ground, and marked on it the railway, the stop named Chifley, the homestead at Mount Singular, and the imagined course of the aircraft.

When he had heard it at Dead Oak Stump, the destination of the aircraft was at one of two points: either to the north of his present camp, or short of his present camp—between it and some place out on the Plain. His position was not less than two hundred miles from the nearest known homestead, Mount Singular. Having recently been able to live off the country, the food in his bags would support him for seven or eight days, when supplies could be replenished at Bumblefoot Hole.

Before sleeping, he decided to prospect the desert for four days, after which he would be compelled to turn back and travel south along that imagined line of flight of the aircraft.

Having to cover as much country as possible in those four days, he was leading his camels off the Plain and high into the dunes before the sun was up, and luck favoured him, only to withdraw the gift within two hours.

He was prompted to halt his camel train and look rearward over the great Plain, the sun not yet risen, and the morning air like crystal, the far edge of the Plain like the lip of a tall cliff one sees from a mere hundred yards back. Then his roving eyes abruptly stilled, to become a stare to annihilate distance.

Crows, a dozen of them, so far away as to appear to be ink-blots. A dead rabbit? A dead kangaroo? Neither. Oh! for a pair of binoculars! Something was surely moving out there, the opposite of the black crows. It was white. Like a white crow but couldn't be. It was like a white handkerchief, being waved to attract his attention.

Down again on the lower elevation of the Plain, he could

...o longer see even the crows. This mattered not at all. Lucy went ahead as usual, thrusting into the gentle south wind. The camels followed the walking man, happy to have their faces turned homeward.

Yet the happiness continued not for long. They had proceeded for a mile, and now Bony could see the crows and the white object of their interest when Millie tugged back on her noseline, and he halted to see what was wrong. He could find nothing wrong. He could see nothing to excite them. The ground was firm. Impatiently he called to them and went on.

Another half mile, and they did come to an area indicating subterranean cavities. He had to select a twisting passage to avoid the bare rock and to keep to the close growing saltbush.

The white object fluttered above the ground. It wasn't a handkerchief, but was certainly fabric of some kind. Not yet could he determine the agency keeping it in motion.

Minutes later he knew what the white object was—a silk scarf, and it was poised by an uprush of air from a blow-hole precisely like a ball on a water-jet in a shooting gallery.

To be bothered with the whys at this time was to wool-gather. To be bothered with fractious camels was equally waste of time. He took the throwing ropes from his saddle and spent less than three minutes in roping both animals so that they couldn't rise from their knees.

With the rifle he caught the fluttering scarf and drew it from the air current. It was of fine quality silk. It bore no initials, but was certainly a woman's scarf. When he peered into the blow-hole, the air beat upon his face. He sniffed, and the smell baffled him. He could detect only that the odour was not entirely composed of damp rock and water, bats, or the smell of any burrowing rodent. Coffee? No! Surely not coffee?

Leaving the blow-hole, he prospected. Lucy began to bark. The warning chill at Bony's neck made him turn about. The crows appeared to have lost their reason; there was nothing he could see. He circled the blow-hole, and so found the large hole five feet in diameter and about centre of flat bare limestone rock.

Behind him Lucy barked furiously, and he turned quickly, the chill on the neck now of ice.

He was confronted by four wild aborigines. Each was aiming a spear tipped with flint, the butt resting in the socket of a throwing stick. Their faces were impassive. Their eyes were wide and steady, like their bodies, their arms, their weapons.

Chapter Nine

ADVERSITY IS BUT A SPUR

LEAVES and fine twigs were entwined with the wild men's hair, and damp earth clung to their knees and chests. The stalking of their quarry had been accomplished with the perfection of the greatest masters on earth.

Cicatrices on faces and chests and thighs proved full initiation into the Luritja Nation, the remnants of which still occupy the Central Desert. They were small, incredibly tough, and had the endurance of the dingo. Their hair was bunched high by a band of snake-skin, that of three being black, that of the fourth being grey, and matching the straggly beard. He was a medicine man.

The condition of thighs and stomachs indicated they were living on white man's food. Oddity number one. Oddity number two was the unacceptable coincidence that they delayed appearance until Bony was looking at the large entrance to a cavern.

He could have employed the rifle, could have shot one, but only one, before he himself fell to the spears of the others. The formula: "I am Inspector Bonaparte, and I arrest you for . . ." was so much piffling eye-wash in this situation. Obviously it was not their intention to kill him and make off with the food and gear; otherwise their spears would now be halfway through his body.

The medicine man, who was the natural leader, beckoned him forward, and when he complied, the others slipped around behind him and continued on until they were with the camels, and then the medicine man held out a hand for the rifle, and motioned Bony to sit on the ground. There he was as much a captive as though weighed with a hundred-weight of manacles.

Eyes glittered but the spears remained poised while Bony removed his coat and shirt. They remained like sculptured figures at a white man's exhibition as he gained his feet and slowly turned about for them to see the cicatrices on his own back, he blessing old Chief Illawarrie of the far north, who had inducted him into the Mysteries of the Alchuringa Days.

What astonished them was that he, who was not wholly of their race, had been sealed into a Nation of the Ancient People. The leader spoke to the others, but they remained silent and made no sign. As intended by Bony, the situation became complicated, and often engineered complications will save such a tight situation.

The leader became human. From his dillybag of kan-garoo skin, suspended from his neck by human hair, he produced a plug of tobacco and bit a chew. Bony dressed, squatted on his heels, and proceeded to roll a cigarette. The camels were no longer nervous, and Lucy lay beside Millie and watched. The warriors squatted, their spears on the ground beside them. Their prisoner was safe enough. Any one of them could have pinned Bony within seconds, and all his knowledge of ju-jitsu would have been of no avail. They had one superlative trick, and the thought of it made him wiggle his toes.

"What for you fellers do this?" he asked, and was surprised when the leader said:

"Wa for you come here, eh? You tell."

Mission contact! Hermansburg, perhaps! Ooldea . . . before the great Daisy Bates had to give up . . . a visitor, perhaps, to Ooldea just long enough to gain a smattering of English.

"Dingoes," replied Bony. "Patsy Lonergan my father and my uncle. Patsy Lonergan . . . you know Patsy Lonergan?"

The name registered. They spoke softly among themselves.

"Patsy Lonergan die quick," he told them, and nodded to the camels. "I get Patsy Lonergan's camels. Now I catch dingoes."

Further soft interchange of opinions among them lasted a full minute. No reference had been made to the silk scarf which they must have seen fluttering above the blow-hole, and which they must have seen being crammed into a pocket. Finally two of the young men rose and proceeded to unload the camels, taking no notice of Lucy's barks of protest. The unloading completed, they removed Millie's noseline, and, despite Curley's objection, removed his leather halter. The ropes holding them down were removed and the animals were kicked to their feet and sent running. The leader shouted an order, and one of the men seized Lucy and the other bound her with the noseline.

The ropes were then securely knotted and one end fastened about Bony's chest. The unloading and freeing of the camels was puzzling him, and fastening the rope about him seemed for the purpose of conducting him to their camp, although even this was unnecessary.

The leader now motioned him to walk to the area of bare rock in the centre of which was the gaping opening of the cavern, and about this he could do nothing but obey. A few moments later he knew their intention was to lower him into the cavern. At the edge of the hole he turned in rebellion, and the leader, without emotion, said:

"Better you go with rope. Long way."

Wisdom, if of sinister import. The great Inspector

Bonaparte realised, when encountering those four pairs of relentless eyes, that it would be wise to accept the assistance of the rope as the floor of the cavern could be more than a few feet under the ground surface. Thus, without injury, he found himself on the floor of limestone, approximately twenty feet below the surface.

He was in a chamber roughly circular, and something like thirty feet in diameter, the walls curving inward as they mounted to the orifice. The limestone floor was uneven. He saw the mouth of what appeared to be a long tunnel, down which burned a star of light. To one side, on a wide rock ledge stood low stacks of tinned food. There was an opening off this place, and, of all objects to quicken his amazement, he could see a large kerosene stove.

Then those above were jerking at the rope, requiring him to free himself of it. This he did, and they drew it up.

He could hear Lucy barking up top. From the tunnel issued a voice slightly distorted by echo, saying:

"I didn't do it! Damn you all, I didn't do it!"

It could have been Ganba, only Ganba is known to ignore English. Besides, Ganba doesn't need a light to aid him on his underground gallivanting.

It came again like the same voice, the words disproving it.

"You done it all right, you stinking rat."

Movement above again drew Bony's attention. The opening was being masked by Curley's pack-saddle, and he had to leap aside to avoid it. After it, came the riding saddle, the pack-bags, and every item of his gear, including even the camel bells and the hobbles, everything save the rifle. The resultant clatter had no effect on the voice or voices, down the tunnel.

"You waited for him and smashed him with a rock. I didn't, I tell you! I didn't! Oh, leave him alone."

Up above, a new sound, Lucy's frightened whimpering.

69

She was being lowered by the rope, and when Bony caught her, the rope was drawn up. She licked his face happily as he swiftly unbound her.

"Sure he's dead, Mark?" said the tunnel. "My dear Myra, of course he's dead."

The recollection of the automatic pistol was one of a chaotic sequence. The wild men had spent no time with the gear and his effects, other than to strip the camels and toss everything down after him, everything save that beautiful Savage rifle and the loading ropes. They would drive the camels away, and even now might well be engaged in brushing out their tracks to complete the obliteration of all evidence leading to the discovery of this place.

As the dramatist might say, it wasn't in character. Most decidedly it was unorthodox. The possession of tobacco proved recent contact with whites. These people in that tunnel—who were they, what were they doing here? Myra Thomas! Who else? But prisoners, as he assuredly was. Those saddle-bags which contained his personal effects contained his own automatic.

He fell upon the bags, dragging them from under one of the water drums, swiftly unstrapped the off-side bag and delved for the weapon, small and compact, and deadly at twenty feet. He knew that the clip was full. A broken box of cartridges he slipped into another pocket, and the bag was re-strapped and tossed back to the heap of gear littering the floor.

A voice in the tunnel said:

"Why, here's a ruddy dog!"

All English so far. No guttural voices. Lucy had found them.

"That's funny. How the hell did she get here? Must be someone up top. Come on! If she got in, we oughta get out."

The light twinkled. It was being carried along the

tunnel. Seated on the heap of his gear, Bony waited. The sunlight through the opening was falling slightly to his rear making him conscious of the fact that he occupied the commanding position in this situation now developing.

"She's a pet dog," a woman said in the tunnel. "She loves being made a fuss of. What's your name, sweet?"

A man entered the chamber followed by the woman, then four men. They halted at the tunnel's mouth, appearing to Bony as ghosts lurking in a cobweb-festooned corner of a derelict dungeon. The woman held the wriggling dog, only her shape indicative of her sex, for she wore men's trousers and coat over a man's sports shirt. The man carrying the hurricane lantern was tall and hawk-faced. Another was big and muscular. A shrimp of a man peered with weak eyes, and another seemed to have springs in his knees.

Every face was putty white, faces in which eyes glowed like dull coals in a dark room. They stood there staring at the stranger seated on the pile of gear, as though utterly unable to believe what they were seeing, until it seemed to Bony that in this tableau only the dog moved.

The woman released the dog, who ran to Bony and snuggled against him. Bony said, politely:

"How d'you do?"

They came forward, slowly, led by the woman. The tall man's face was insulted by the clothes he wore, for the sweeping breadth of the forehead, the mane of iron-grey hair, the cast of the mouth, and the expression in his dark eyes pictured intelligence above the average. His voice supported what his countenance portrayed.

"Who are you?" he asked, with the 'old' school accent.

Bony recognised him.

"The name is William Black."

"It conveys nothing, Mr. Black. How did you come to be here?"

71

'Dumped by wild aborigines."

"Wild aborigines! How extraordinary. What are those things you are sitting on?"

"Camel gear."

"Camel gear! Camels! Wild aborigines! Whom did you murder?"

The light-blue eyes were compelling, the eyes of a man accustomed to being obeyed. He was, Bony was aware, Dr. Carl Havant, a psychiatrist who practised in Sydney until eleven years ago.

"I cannot recall having murdered anyone," Bony replied.

"I am still doubtful. What school did you attend?"

Ah! Clever indeed is the man who can adopt a fictitious character and maintain it under sudden stress. He had spoken in his usual manner.

"Never mind about that," he said sharply. "Who are you, and what are you all doing here?"

"We are merely in residence." The tall man regarded Bony gravely. "Would you oblige by telling us precisely where our residence is, we presume, in Australia?"

"We are now on the northern extremity of the Nullarbor Plain."

"There, Maddoch! Did I not argue that we must be on the Nullarbor Plain?"

The dark eyes looked down upon the short man whose clothes hung upon him, and who appeared emotionally bankrupt. The man with the knees like springs answered for the little man.

"Could have been east Gippsland, like Clifford said. Could have been up north a bit from Perth, like I told you."

"Yes, yes! Quite. Well, we are at the north of the Nullarbor Plain. And now, Mr. Black. You tell us that you were 'dumped'—your own word—down here by wild aborigines. I've always thought that wild aborigines are to be found only in the north of Australia. Pardon repetition. Whom did you murder? Please do not hesitate, Mr. Black, or be alarmed."

"Caw" exploded the man with the springy legs, "I know this Mister Black now. I'd bet on it. Doc, and ladies and gents, meet Inspector Napoleon Bonaparte."

Chapter Ten

BONY IS HONOURED

THEY were young and deeply in love. He was a tally clerk on the wharves, and she worked in a city shop. They were saving to build a home, but in these days it takes a long time to meet the rising costs of building.

So Nature won. Their dream was a home, not a hasty marriage and return to the parental country home. Only in the city could they earn 'real' money. Eventually, following much discussion, the man talked with another, who suggested the name of a woman; the girl consulted the helpful nurse who arranged her admittance to a private 'hospital', together with a goodly proportion of the money they had saved.

It was all very mysterious. Shortly after, the body was found in a ditch fifty miles out of town, the young tally clerk was interviewed by a detective and taken to the morgue to identify his sweetheart. He was asked where the operation had been performed, and he explained that a taxi had called for the girl at the shop at close of business. This was in accordance with agreement made by the girl with someone of whom he knew nothing.

He admitted that he knew the girl's intention to enter a hospital, but nothing beyond this. The taxi-driver came forward to report that he had picked up the girl outside the shop, having received instructions by radio from his garage. The garage manager said that the instructions were the result of a telephone call.

At the passenger's request, the driver had put his fare down in the main street of an outer suburb. The girl paid the charge. He took particular notice of her because she was pretty, and was obviously under a great strain. Then by a quirk of fate his engine stopped, and he had to tinker with it. It was while doing so that a private car stopped and collected the girl. He remembered the car because it was a late model Lagonda. He remembered, too, the registration number.

The Lagonda was owned by Doctor Carl Havant.

So Doctor Carl Havant, the well-known psychiatrist, was charged with murder, found guilty of manslaughter, sentenced to ten years.

That was in 1947, and now in 1956 he was with Inspector Bonaparte in a cavern under the Nullarbor Plain. Even with the normal remissions for good conduct, the dates seemed wrong.

"Inspector of what?" asked Dr. Havant, and Edward Jenks of the springy knees chortled:

"Detective-Inspector, of course."

Edward Jenks was thirty-five and employed as cook on a small station property when Bony arrested him. Now he looked over sixty. He was of middle height, thick-set, still powerful, and his large head was set on a short thick neck. A sailor ashore in Brisbane, he had been bilked one night by a prostitute, which so annoyed him that subsequently he waylaid her for the satisfaction of strangling her. The death sentence having been abolished in Queensland, he was sentenced to life, but had served only nine years when released on parole.

"A detective-inspector" echoed Dr. Havant, and the woman laughed with a hint of hysteria. "And Bonaparte is the name. Happy to meet you, Inspector Bonaparte. I'm sure we are all glad you have found us."

The sunlight was now funnelling directly upon Bony who still sat at apparent ease on the mass of his gear. The doctor's face, and that of another, had the cretaceous quality of chalk. They had shaved quite recently. A tall man who looked to be about thirty had cultivated a brown vandyke beard, and in the shadows the little nervous man looked old and ill.

Mere impressions. The figures were tense, the least taut being the woman. Her hands were well kept, and her hair neatly coiled and pinned. Bony recalled the voices deep in the tunnel, and decided to take control of a situation which neither they nor he could yet understand.

"Are you Myra Thomas?" he asked.

"I am," she replied calmly. "You should know that."

"You must admit to your identity."

"Of course. Sorry, Inspector."

"I have been looking for you."

The psychiatrist-abortionist chuckled, then sniffed.

"Do I smell coffee, Myra?"

"You do. But there's a body if anyone is interested. I was preparing breakfast when Igor was killed."

The little man began denial of something, and the man with the vandyke beard began to talk him down, when the doctor loudly ordered silence. A huge fellow now inserted himself into Bony's notice by saying:

"Have some common. This bloke's a d. Blimey! Do we want trouble piled on? Gimme the lamp, Mark. I'll fix the business."

"It can wait, Joe, till we sort of straighten things," Vandyke said impatiently. "Forget the d. He can't do anything. We'll have breakfast and let him tell us how he came here, and what he intends doing now he is here."

"Quite " murmured Havant. "Breakfast, Myra. Coffee."

They dispersed. The woman and Jenks faded into the natural annexe where Bony had seen the large kerosene stove. Vandyke said:

"I'll give you a hand to shift this stuff to one side, Inspector. The name's Brennan, Mark Brennan."

What *was* all this? Mark Brennan! Bony glanced sharply at him, and encountered light-blue eyes, steady and candid.

Mark Brennan! Bony knew the name and the circumstances, and created a picture from what he had read:

The golden shafts of sunlight poured upon the little church set amid encircling gums a few miles from Orange, New South Wales. The small crowd outside the main door could hear the Wedding March. The year was 1939, and the military camps were beginning to accept volunteers.

Among the people outside the church was a young man in uniform, not yet accustomed to wearing it. Beside him were several other young men, obviously a little envious of his attraction for the girls who cast admiring glances at him as they waited to see the bride. The young man was the son of a local storekeeper, and now on his first leave.

Others watched him with covert curiosity, for inside the church his one-time sweetheart was being married—to his rival of long standing. He stood there, hands in pockets, the loose stance of the recruit already seeing himself a veteran.

Out upon the low porch stepped the bride and groom, well matched, beautiful in youth, blessed by the vows they had exchanged. They came down the porch steps and people began tossing confetti at them.

Mark Brennan did not throw confetti. From his military coat he drew a pistol and shot the bride between the eyes. The groom was almost dragged to the ground by her lifeless body. Then, with one arm about her, he straightened and

77

confronted the murderer—who shot him in the stomach.

The case caused wide public interest. Tragic young man! Torn apart by duty to his country, and grieved by the loss of his sweetheart. The jury recommended mercy. The judge passed the death sentence. The Executive Council automatically commuted the sentence to life imprisonment, and marked his papers: *Never To Be Released*.

Never to be released! And here he was assisting Bony to move his gear to the side of the cavern under the Nullarbor Plain. The beard made him look arty, and handsome. The eyes were cold, as they must have been when he pressed the trigger of the pistol, twice.

The chore accomplished, Bony sat on Curley's saddle and rolled a cigarette. Watchful, he waited for these riddles to be solved. A cloth of clean canvas had been spread on the rock floor, and on this the woman was placing sliced baking powder bread, opened tins of sardines, a bottle of sauce, a tin of jam.

The man Jenks appeared with a jug of coffee and a fruit tin of sugar. He filled tin pannikins with coffee, and Mark Brennan said:

"Help yourself, Inspector."

Bony returned to his saddle with a pannikin of coffee.

"You have had breakfast, Inspector?" Doctor Havant enquired solicitously.

"Yes, thank you," politely replied Bony.

"You find yourself in a strange community, Inspector; in fact, an unique community. I shall eventually write several books about it, I hope. You know, the effect of complete isolation on the human mind. Also I shall write a thesis on the herd instinct in humans.

"Jenks has spoken much of you, Inspector. He bestows upon you the mantle of Javert, although he has never read Hugo's masterpiece. Entirely in his favour is a lack of animosity towards you, who found him and had him arrested. In that he is unlike our friend there, Joseph Riddell, to whom all policemen are anathema."

Joseph Riddell! Riddell in 1941 was working on a farm near Brisbane. He was then a taciturn man of thirty years, strong, a good worker, and treated with consideration by his employer. One afternoon there arose dissension between them, concerning a head wound suffered by a cow, and that evening Riddell shot his employer dead with a shot-gun belonging to the victim. He vanished with the farmer's car which he abandoned, and stole another, to abandon that also when the petrol gave out.

Eventually caught, he received a sentence of twelve years. Another recommendation for mercy. Lonely unfortunate man, living in a hut on a farm when the farmer and his wife lived in luxury in a fine house. If he had bashed the milking cow, the ruddy boss had no right to jaw him about it! Having served nine years he was freed.

Here was Joseph Riddell, still of powerful physique, his hair and beard barely touched with grey.

Observing Bony looking at him, he leaned back on his haunches and grinned. The grin preceded rumbling laughter.

"Hell! It's damn funny all right," he asserted, voice deep. "By hell, it's funny. You'll be able to write plenty about all this, Doc."

"What's funny about it?" snarled the little man with thin sandy hair and weak eyes. "If he is really a police detective, then he can get us all out of here. There's nothing funny about walking on the earth instead of living like a colony of rats under it."

Emotion raised the voice but did not disguise the accent, and there lingered still in this man's voice the tone of authority. He reminded Bony of someone he had seen

79

pictured in the newspapers, and now Havant gave the picture its name.

"My dear Clifford Maddoch, I am strongly in agreement with Joe that the situation existing at this moment is truly funny. I dislike the word, but repeat it because used by you and Joseph. It is funny, because we of the R.M.I. happen to be at a slight disadvantage precisely when Inspector Bonaparte drops in to bid good morning."

So this was Clifford Maddoch. At the time he had given his wife a measure of strychnine, thallium not then having come into favour for this purpose; he was the manager of an important branch of a wool brokerage firm, the president of the local golf club, and the secretary of the Urban District Committee. For fourteen years he had suffered torture from the battering voice which had probed and pierced the recesses of his mind. It was a strange coincidence that the judge committed him to prison for fourteen years. And having served ten years, he was released.

"You shut up, Clifford," snarled Riddell. "No good you crawling to the Inspector now, after what you just done."

The little man leaped to his feet. It seemed that every nerve in his face began to twitch violently.

"I'm not guilty," he shouted, having to struggle for articulation. "I told you all I didn't do it. I liked Igor Mitski . . . for everything bar his voice."

Bony recalled the case of Igor Mitski, the displaced, the singer, serving his period of grace in Australia on a north-west station in New South Wales. Cultured, able to speak a little English, banished to live with strange people in a strange land. A Polish Jew who had suffered badly.

The employer and his wife were kindly people. Instead of making Mitski a gardener, they appointed him music teacher to their little girl aged eight. Circumstances climbed high and smashed both Mitski and the child. Mitski still mentally wounded by the treatment received from the invaders of his country; the child spoiled and stubborn, as an only child can be. In a rage, Mitski hit her. Released on parole when having served twenty months of the sentence for manslaughter.

Mitski! Bony had been in a far western town when Mitski was tried. He had arrived there on the last day of the trial and was in court when the prisoner was sentenced. A woman had run from the witnesses' seat to the dock, and a man had quickly caught her in his arms and tried to pacify her. Bony hadn't been in court officially, and the incident therefore had not been mentally docketed. He said now:

"Mitski slew a little child."

"That was so, Inspector," replied Doctor Havant. "All here know the history of everyone. We often discuss personal experiences, desires, ambitions, satisfactions. We are, actually, a very conservative body." He chuckled in his dry humourless way, and taking the others into his range, he went on: "I suggest, gentlemen, that we nominate and accept the Inspector into our honoured Association. I have pleasure in putting forward the name of Inspector Bonaparte. I feel that he will do what in him lies to succour and encourage every member, that he will conduct himself worthily, and toil ever on behalf of the defenceless and the unfortunate. What say you?"

"Taking a ruddy risk," growled Riddell. "He don't qualify."

"I propose Inspector Bonaparte," chirped Clifford Maddoch.

"I take pleasure in seconding the proposal, Mr. President," drawled Brennan.

Doctor Havant stood. He beamed on the assembly, and his chalky complexion appeared likely to fall off in flakes. The dark eyes regarding Bony recalled to him the eyes of the woman at Mount Singular. Then he remembered where he had seen her before, and the probability of this extraordinary development was like a star born in his mind. He heard the doctor say:

"Welcome, Inspector Bonaparte, into our exclusive Association. I publicly announce your elevation to a Fellowship of the Released Murderers' Institute."

Chapter Eleven

A BODY FOR BONY

"I APPRECIATE the honour," Bony said gravely. "I have many questions which must wait, and doubtless you have many to ask, but first things first. The body. Take me to it."

"Better arrest this twirp," offered Joseph Riddell. "He hated Igor Mitski 'cos his voice reminded him of his missus. Didn't like Igor singing to us, an' Igor was better than the blasted wireless singers too." Maddoch again shouted his innocence, and when Riddell once more taunted him the girl broke in with:

"That will be all from you, Riddell. You're taking a back seat from now on. You've no proof that Clifford killed Mitski, so keep your silly big mouth closed."

Bony swiftly intervened.

"It would seem that all of you are murderers, that all but one have been convicted and released on licence. Other than not having periodically reported, you are of no official interest to me. But you say you have a dead man on your hands, that he was killed, and you infer that one of you killed him. Where is the body of this man?"

"Jenks! The lamp," said the doctor, adding to Bony: "Jenks is the custodian of the lamps and the oil, which is in short supply."

The ex-sailor struck a match and applied it to the wick of a hurricane lamp. The doctor took it from him and led the way into the tunnel. They could walk upright, and the floor was level. They passed on the left a branch tunnel from which issued a faint moaning sound. The main tunnel entered a chamber, the limits of which the power of the lamp failed to reach. Bony was conducted past a huge boulder which had fallen from the roof, and over a clear space. Havant stopped, and his lamp revealed a man lying on his chest, and a narrow stream of blood extending into the darkness. He was dressed in working clothes, rough and durable.

"He hasn't been moved?" he asked the doctor.

"No. I lifted his head by the hair. The frontal bone has been crushed. Death was obvious, and before I could examine him further, my attention was distracted by the arrival of your dog."

"Turn him over, someone."

Jenks did so, and the woman cried out.

Bony estimated that the dead man was close to six feet in height. The body was reasonably well nourished, the face clean-shaven, and the iron-grey hair clipped short.

"With what was he killed?" asked Bony.

"We don't know," the girl answered. "Probably with a piece of stone."

"We haven't looked for the weapon yet," volunteered Brennan.

"Bring more lights, if you have them. We'll look for it now."

Jenks departed, and Bony watched his departing figure in the tunnel against the daylight at its far end. He asked who found the body, and Mark Brennan said he had found it about half an hour before they discovered the arrival of Bony. When asked under what circumstances, he went on:

"I was with Myra looking for her scarf in the passage leading to the air shaft. We heard Igor shout out something like 'Do not! Do not!' Then he shouted once, 'Help!' I left Myra and ran with our lamp to see what was wrong. I collided with Doctor Havant just as I reached the main passage, and he said he'd been in what we call the hall, so Igor wasn't there. We came here, and met Riddell carrying a lamp and Maddoch was with him."

"Leaves Jenks. What about Jenks?"

"Jenks just turned up to hunt for Mitski with us," replied Brennan. "We looked around here, and I happened to find the body. It's a pretty large place as you can see."

Bony couldn't see until Jenks arrived with three hurricane lamps. The four lamps standing on the boulder enabled him then to see the extremities of this cavern.

"It is obvious, Inspector, that one of us is a murderer," tritely observed Dr. Havant.

"Any other passages leading off this place?"

"One that ends in a cul-de-sac. Another goes down to what we call the Jeweller's Shop, and from there on to what I named Fiddler's Leap."

"Other than those present, there are no more of you?"

"No. One of us killed Mitski with a rock."

"How d'you know it was a rock?"

"Because he was killed with a blunt instrument. We have no blunt instruments other than rocks ranging from small pebbles to the size of this boulder. We have knives, table knives. Mitsky wasn't killed with a table knife."

"In your opinion, Doctor, would the blunt instrument have blood on it?"

"The answer is difficult, Inspector. Probably not if only the one blow was struck; most likely if more than one blow."

Bony bade them stand back, and he spent several minutes looking for the weapon. The floor was entirely clean of debris, and on his mentioning it, he was informed that all debris had long since been removed to the short passage which ended in a cul-de-sac.

"We will return to the place where we met," he said, and the obliging Doctor Havant explained that that had been named the hall.

The return to 'the hall' was welcomed by Bony who felt distinctly uneasy in that eerie cavern. They stood watching him, waiting, as he sat on the pack-saddle and fell to making the inevitable cigarette. Their behaviour was unlike normal people, who would have sought information and explanation, and he wondered what this attitude could mean. He recognised the wisdom of delaying satisfaction of his own curiosity.

"Make yourselves easy," he said. "I'll talk first, and before I begin one of you answer a question. Are you being kept here against your will?"

All spoke at once, and he waved them to silence. That some of them had been imprisoned here for a long time was evidenced by their faces, and a child could have deduced that they would not have remained had they found a way of escape.

"You know who I am, and what I represent," he began. "You know that I am a tracker of men, but you don't know my personal views on crime and criminals.

"I did not frame the laws. Officially, I am not concerned whether a law is sound or futile. Officially, I am not concerned with whatever penalty is imposed for breaking a law. Personally, as a private citizen, I have an abhorrence of murder, the crime which concerns us. To make myself clear, there is another point.

"Each of you men committed a crime and was released when constituted authority chose to think you had been sufficiently punished. Because you did not comply with certain conditions I am able, officially, to prove that you were forcibly prevented from compliance. That isn't a rash statement, for I believe I have the key to the reason behind this enforced detention, if you do not know it. Do you?"

"We do not, Inspector," Havant said.

"We'd ruddy well like to," snorted Riddell.

"We'll pass it for the moment," Bony continued. "I was assigned to find a missing woman known as Myra Thomas, who disappeared from a train. The Police held nothing against her, following her acquittal, but the Police were, and are, interested in her because she is a missing person. You are all missing persons, and it is the duty of every policeman to search for such.

"I set out to look for Myra Thomas, and eventually was led to this place by the aid of several clues, including her scarf. Having located her, I would have freed you also, had I not been found wanting in wariness. As I see it now, I am one with you, a prisoner. I have no doubt that you have tried many times to find a way to freedom, and with the introduction of my fresh mind, we may solve this problem.

"Now for the crux of future relations between you and me. If anything happened to me, and eventually you found a way of escape from this hole, you would never find your way back to civilisation, even if you were not hunted down by the persons who brought you here, or by their agents. We are now more than two hundred miles from the nearest homestead, and in the most relentlessly hostile country in Australia.

"So that, as convicted murderers, you may have strong animosity toward me, a police officer, but you must realise that even at this stage you are dependent on me to get you out from this hole and back to civilisation. To employ a nautical cliché, we sink or swim together."

"I'm not swimmin'," growled Riddell.

Myra Thomas would have spoken had not Dr. Havant turned to stare at the gorilla. He said, quietly:

"Riddell."

"I don't aim . . ."

"Riddell, I am reading your thoughts."

Riddell's eyes avoided Havant. He looked at his naked feet, and his huge body seemed to shrink. Bony had never seen a human being so quickly reduced to abjectness. There was no threat expressed in the doctor's words or by his face, yet his domination was supreme. Bony, feeling the sudden tension, asserted himself.

"Two tasks confront me," he told them. "To apprehend those who have unlawfully restricted your freedom; the other, to apprehend the slayer of Igor Mitski."

"I hope you get him, Inspector," declared the girl who had been acquitted of murder. "He never harmed anyone here." Stooping, she gathered the breakfast things, and as she conveyed them to the annexe she added: "And don't think that because one of you killed Igor that the rest of you now have a chance."

"You can't never tell," Jenks said. "Hey, Doc, some day you'll be able to write a book called *Make Mine Women*."

"You won't be in it, Ted," drawled Mark Brennan.

"Says you, Mark. We'll all be in it. The wench has been looking for strife ever since she came here. She likes strife, she does. S'why she bumped off her husband."

"All right! All right! Think of something else."

The girl came from the annexe and gathered the remainder of the breakfast things, pausing to look down contemptuously at the ex-sailor, who was seated on the floor with his back to the rock bench. The resultant action by Jenks was so swift that Bony was barely able to follow it. Jenks shot forward and gripped her ankle, pulled. The action of her fall was slow motion by comparison with his.

Bony rose to his feet, as body after body piled on top of Jenks and the girl until there was a heap of fighting lunatics. Dr. Havant crossed to Bony's side, waved him back to his seat on the saddle. He said:

"It's nothing, Inspector. Like water over a fire which must eventually come to the boil. I have found it essential in order to maintain a modicum of sanity to permit the steam to escape. While they fight over the woman, they won't fight us."

"But the woman, she'll be hurt," objected Bony.

"Be not distressed," urged Havant, icily calm. "She came up the slum way, and it sticks to her and always will, despite the veneer of education."

Myra Thomas was now trying hard to sink her teeth into Jenks's arm, as he did his utmost to pull her scalp off, gripping her hair with a hand trained to grip rope. Mark Brennan was hammering Jenks with one fist, and with the other attempted to flatten Riddell's navel against his backbone. To counter this, the big man was pulling Brennan's hair upward with one hand, and his vandyke beard downward with the other.

When little Maddoch appeared with a can of boiling water, the doctor called to him, shook his head disapprovingly, and Maddoch's reaction was to shrug his narrow shoulders and trot back to the annexe with the dampener. It was extraordinary that he heard the doctor's voice above the shouts, yells, and screams. Returning, Maddoch came carefully round the human heap, and to Bony he said with mouth close:

"It's the cavern, Inspector. They behave like this now and then, but more often when the woman is around. She's an unsettling influence."

"A truthful and original statement," drily agreed Havant. "You know, Inspector, human hair has remarkable tensile strength to withstand assault. The girl started this fracas. I think she enjoys it, although at the moment one must admit to being faintly alarmed by her present predicament."

There was, however, no cause for perturbation. The girl suddenly extricated herself from the tangled mass, her violet eyes glittering with triumph. She smiled defiantly at both Havant and Bony, handed Jenks a right smart face slap, lifted a blanket revealing a second annexe, and disappeared.

Brennan sat up and tenderly combed his beard with his fingers, as though needing assurance that he still had one. The others rose unsteadily, and sheepishly inspected the damage.

With the cessation of violence there was silence.

Unnoticed, the dog had departed.

Chapter Twelve

ARTHUR FIDDLER'S WAY OUT

OF these men, Bony judged Clifford Maddoch to be the least dangerous, the most sane. With the exception of Maddoch and Doctor Havant, they were now licking their wounds, and Havant he told firmly to remain with them.

Again he stood beside the remains of Igor Mitski, manipulating the lamp, and on the far side of the body Maddoch watched and waited.

"A severe blow," Bony said. "And if a rock was the weapon, it must have been fairly large and heavy."

"I didn't do this, Inspector," the little man cried, desperately. "I couldn't kill anyone . . . not like that. Mitski was a fine man. I could talk to him even though his main interest was music and I know little about it. He could sing too, and even make music from a row of tin pannikins. I had no cause to kill him."

"You disliked his voice," murmured Bony.

"Only when he became excited," admitted Maddoch, "then his voice resembled that of my wife . . . her riveting voice . . . I can hear it even now. But I'm not a real murderer. I couldn't hurt anyone. I don't believe you could understand, but Igor did. You see, after the Russians invaded his country they locked a metal thing over his head and beat it with a bar, and the noise almost drove him mad. So he knew what I had to suffer for years and years before I simply had to do something about it. I didn't really murder

91

my wife, not in my mind I didn't, but I had to stop that voice from crawling into my head like a talking maggot."

No, he couldn't hurt his wife by knocking her down. He didn't hurt her when he slipped poison into her glass of sherry, although the poison did. Every policeman knows that some persons are natural murderers, but the Law will not accept that in extenuation. So Bony must persist.

"When excited, Mitski's voice did irritate you," he pressed.

"Yes, it did. I used to beg of him to be calm. His voice didn't go on and on for hours like my wife's did, when I could have screamed for sleep, yet didn't dare occupy another room."

"Where were you when Mitski shouted 'Do not! Do not! Help!'?"

"I was coming from the Jeweller's Shop where I'd been to empty kitchen waste down a shaft," replied Maddoch. "I know the way so well that I didn't need a light, and oil is precious. I heard Igor call out just before I left the passage to this cavern, and when I entered it, I saw movement just here. Whatever it was—I didn't know then what it was—it stopped as I went towards it and I could see nothing. As I was groping past that big boulder, I heard someone behind me and Riddell grabbed me, and the others were all here."

"You say you were without a light. Where was the light in this cavern when you saw movement?"

"I didn't need a light."

"Then how could you see movement in the dark?"

"I'll show you how it is, Inspector. I'll stay here. You go over there and blow out the lamp."

Bony accepted the suggestion. Having puffed out the lamp, he waited for his eyes to become accustomed to the darkness when he found that the light from the distant 'hall' gave just sufficient illumination to see the formless figure standing beside the body, and the boulder which was several feet to the left.

"Wave your arms," he ordered, and the little man did so. Having re-lit the lamp, he called to Maddoch to join him.

"What is your height?"

"Five feet seven, Inspector."

"Your age?"

"Fifty-four."

"Now show me the rest of this place."

Maddoch conducted him to a short off-passage ending in a cul-de-sac, explaining that once it had been used as a dump, and was now the site of a tunnel being driven by Jenks, who thought this was the only way out.

"He's been working here for a long time," Maddoch said, indicating a hole roughly wide enough to take Riddell's larger frame. Bony peered into the hole, seeing that the tunnel had been excavated for less than six feet. "All he had to dig with was a table knife, which is why the table knives are worn halfway and to a point. When he broke two off at the handle, the doctor made him stop."

There was so much in Bony's mind clamouring for elucidation, but he schooled himself to concentrate on the dead man, and the plan of this underground labyrinth.

"All right, Maddoch, go ahead."

There was an annexe off this cavern which his guide said was the largest, and was evidently the sleeping quarters of the five surviving men. This concluded the points of interest here, and Maddoch then led the way down a sloping passage having a rough floor, and not wide enough to permit two persons to pass. Following many twists and sharp turns, they came to what Maddoch announced was The Jeweller's Shop.

The light carried by Maddoch was reflected to them from a million points. The chamber was so crowded with chandelier stalactites meeting with stalagmites rising from the floor that these columns of calcium carbonate formed fluted drapery, fashioned organ pipes of pearl, even the jaws of sharks, mysterious grottoes and implements of torture.

"Look. I'll show you," cried Maddoch, a note of ecstasy in his thin voice which echoed as though by a giant. Stepping behind the columns he waved the lamp, and the columns shimmered in pearl and silver, and caused to be born and instantly die a myriad of bright bars. The roof was filled with stars, winking as the light moved. The little man continued in the role of Aladdin in his vast and glorious treasure house, and had to be brought to earth by Bony, who wished to know if the running water, flowing into a great basin and slowly spilling over to cascade into a shaft, was their water supply.

"Yes, Inspector. There used to be fish in it—before I came. Igor said he played with them, and was sorry when Fiddler caught and cooked them. They didn't have eyes, and were a dull white colour, and not very palatable."

A passage beyond this cavern was less easy to traverse. It was never of the same width, often being so narrow that Bony wondered if Riddell had negotiated it. It sank abruptly, and at the bottom of the incline they had to crawl under a rock over-hang where claustrophobia would have been distinctly unpleasant. From this point the passage rose slightly, often sharply angled, and ended at yet another cavern the shape of which required a few moments to discern.

This was actually a long compartment where they found themselves on a broad ledge above a wide crack in the floor. Beyond the crack was a similar ledge, and at the rear of this ledge faint daylight revealed the mouth of another passage, which, before the earth had split, had been a continuation of the passage they had come by.

The place was filled with sound. Water gushed, and from the wide crack came the distant roar of water, and another sound to give one pause to consider whether Ganba after all might not be just aboriginal legend.

Maddoch stepped to the edge of the chasm, waved his lamp over it in invitation to Bony to join him and gaze downward, but Bony declined, for he was not yet completely sure of Mr. Clifford Maddoch.

"You don't like heights," Maddoch said. "I don't either, but sometimes I force myself to do something I dislike. How wide d'you think this black gulf is?"

"The light makes it sheer guessing. Perhaps ten feet."

"Quite a jump anyway," Maddoch conceded. "Fiddler made it—one way. Shall we rest and smoke? D'you remember Fiddler?"

They sat with their backs to the wall and their feet were then a couple of yards or more from the lip of the chasm. Bony began with tobacco and paper, and Maddoch produced a table knife, worn almost to the handle and having a long point, with which he cut tobacco from a plug.

"I remember his case in part," Bony replied. "But you tell me."

"I didn't know Fiddler, but since being here, what I know of him I learned from Mitski—that he was overbearing and often unpleasant.

"Arthur Fiddler must have been unbalanced. Early in his career he served jail terms, and then when he was in his early thirties and working as a steeple-jack, his workmate fell and was killed. Fiddler took over the widow and her two children. He could have married the woman, but didn't.

"It seems that he cared for this family commendably for two years, when the woman left him and the two young children. Then, you remember, he gassed the children via the kitchen stove, and only escaped death with them through a miracle of medical science. The usual thing, you know, death sentence, commuted to life, and released on parole after having served eleven years.

"When he was brought here, Igor Mitski had spent ten months alone, for Mitski was the first to be brought here, and the coming of Fiddler saved his sanity. Fiddler was an agile man, as a steeple-jack would be, and he discussed with Igor the possibility of jumping across to the other side to see if that daylight over there meant escape.

"Like us, they could see that the far ledge is slightly lower than this one, and we agreed that the distance between is ten feet, but, as you will also see, the place from which to make the leap is narrow, too narrow to jump with confidence, I'd say.

"Anyway, Arthur Fiddler decided to do it, backing into the passage to extend his run, and Mitski standing right at the edge with the lamp to guide his take off.

"Fiddler made it to the far side. He shouted back at Igor, who cheered his effort, and then he went into the far passage in which he disappeared. Igor waited for Fiddler to return, and when he did, the oil in the lamp had given out. Fiddler shouted that there was nothing above—not a house, a cultivated field or a road of any kind. The land was as flat as a pancake all the way to the horizon on every side, except- ing to the north, where he could see sand dunes. He said they must be on Mars. He had gone a little way from the exit and then realised he might never find the hole again, so he had taken off his shirt, which happened to be white, and laid it over a low bush to guide him back. But after going a mile towards the sand dunes, he found that if he went any farther he wouldn't see the shirt, and so he had returned.

"Igor said he was very excited, and talked like a man who had been badly frightened. He wanted to jump back to what now was safety, but had to wait until Igor refuelled the lamp. He was still there when Igor came back, but appeared to be losing his nerve and said that the return jump looked much more difficult than the first.

"They tried to find a way for Igor to assist him, but there was none. Finally Fiddler said he would delay no longer, and so Igor placed the lamp at the edge of the chasm and Fiddler took his run from the widest part he could find. Well, he missed the ledge by only a few inches, and Igor could do nothing to help him. And so Fiddler fell to his death and Igor was left alone for another five months, when Dr. Havant was brought here."

"There's no way down that cleft, I suppose?" asked Bony.

"No. And it's a long way down to the water. One can count seven slowly before hearing a stone splash."

"Who came after Dr. Havant?"

"I did. Then Brennan and after him Riddell. After Riddell came Jenks. The girl came but a little while ago. I don't know exactly when. We've given up counting days. What's that?"

Into the narrow circle of light entered Lucy, tail wagging her pleasure at finding them.

"I had forgotten about the little dog. Hadn't you?" Maddoch cried, hugging Lucy against his chest.

"Yes . . . and no," confessed Bony. "Tell me what happened to you, the manner in which you were brought here."

"Well, in a way, it was just the same as the others, Inspector. One of the conditions under which I was released was that I was to go at once and remain on a small station property owned by my brother. I was on the way by train, when a woman who was travelling with a man in the same compartment asked me if I were Clifford Maddoch, and when I admitted it, the man said they were delighted to meet me as they were near neighbours of my brother, who had told them I would be on that train.

"I thought it was very decent of them because, after being imprisoned for several years, the outside world is a little frightening. When the train reached a junction, where it halted for twenty minutes, the man suggested that he and I might like to stretch our legs. So we did this, and, quite naturally, both of us walked towards the lavatory, which, as at most railway stops, was at the far end of the platform, and beyond the platform lights.

"As I was about to enter the lavatory, I was struck from behind, and from then on it was all sleeping, and dreaming I was on a truck going somewhere, and not caring where. I remember being lifted from the truck—it could have been a car—and then a sense of being lifted off the ground, and a louder sound was all about me like air. When I did come to my senses, I was lying on blankets in what we call the hall, being given coffee by Dr. Havant, and Igor Mitski was kneeling beside me."

"Can you describe the man and the woman on the train?"

"Yes. The man, or the woman, or both, had a part in kidnapping all of us. The woman was dark and of slight build. She smiled often, but never with her eyes, and Myra Thomas reminds me of her. The man was slightly built but wiry and active. He had dark hair and dark eyes, too. He talked a lot, I seem to remember, but am not clear on this."

"You would know them again?"

"Oh, yes. I would surely know them again, Inspector," answered Clifford Maddoch, and the harshness, the brittle hatred, shocked Bony.

Chapter Thirteen

BONY NOMINATES AN ALLY

"NOW, Maddoch," Bony said, "relax and let me think."

Including Arthur Fiddler, and Igor Mitski who lay dead and still unburied, seven men convicted of murder and sentenced to long terms of imprisonment had been released, abducted and conveyed to these caverns. And a woman who had been acquitted of the charge of murder also had been abducted and brought here.

In every case the release was effected before the expiration of the sentence imposed by the court. In one case, that of Mark Brennan, the prisoner had been released despite his papers having been marked *Never To Be Released*. The ethics of these persons in authority in subverting the sentence imposed by the constituted court was a matter of no official concern to a police officer.

Facts were what Bony sought. The apprehension of law-breakers was his job, and this he often reiterated. The channels through which political influences could work to achieve the release of any of the seven murderers were unknown to him, and, in any case, were not in his territory.

Of official concern to him was that these seven convicted murderers on being released were re-imprisoned without the authority of the State, and in a place not authorised by the State. These men were made free citizens although bound for a period by certain conditions, and that they had not abided by the conditions had been due to circumstances wholly beyond their control.

Within days of release, each had been coshed or drugged, conveyed hundreds of miles by road, then most likely by air and lowered into these caverns where living conditions were far worse than those ruling in a modern Australian jail.

They were provided with food, tinned and dehydrated, a stove to cook the food, and oil to maintain half a dozen lamps. They were given straw-stuffed mattresses and blankets and the common medical remedies but the doctor among them was refused any instruments. Although not denied bare necessities, including hair-cutters and safety razors, they were denied replacement of footwear and mental food by way of books and papers.

The delivery of supplies was irregular and once, for a period of five days, they had been without kerosene for the stove and lamps, following which Jenks had been appointed custodian of the fuel and light stocks. By what type of transport they and the supplies had been conveyed, the prisoners were not in agreement, one saying that even in his drugged state he believed he saw the lifting blades of a helicopter; and another thought he had been brought all the way by truck. At times, when supplies only were brought, they thought it must be by truck, judging by the noise of the engine, but on this point Bony was sure that transportation had been by aircraft.

"Tell me," he said, "just what occurs when supplies are delivered."

"They always come at night," replied Maddoch. "We hear them coming—the engine I mean—long before it actually gets here. The first thing that happens is that a powerful torch is switched on and directed down into the hall. Then a man says: 'All of you below, show yourselves.'

Maybe the reason for that is to prove how many of us are still alive. A long time ago, Doctor Havant objected to this, and was told that the supplies would be estimated on the number of prisoners showing themselves. The doctor continued to object, and no one showed himself. Then no supplies were lowered, and we were on short rations and practically starving when they came again.

"Since then we all show ourselves. The stuff is lowered in sacks, and the oil comes in steel containers holding four gallons. The empty cans are hauled up. Once Jenks caught hold of the rope and attempted to climb up by it, but he was told he was asking to be knocked on the head. Another time Mitski held the rope and refused to let it be drawn up. The men above fired a warning shot, and that settled that."

According to Maddoch, boredom was their greatest enemy, especially when convinced there was no possible escape excepting by the chasm which had claimed Fiddler. After him, no one had dared it, partly because in their minds was the story related to them of Fiddler's terror of the isolation above.

Doctor Havant had a profound influence on Igor Mitski, whom he joined, and on those to come after. Maddoch averred that Dr. Havant saved them from degenerating to the level of animals. He had hypnotic powers of a kind which could subdue Riddell and Jenks, but not Mitski, Brennan or the girl. Maddoch said he could resist Havant's hypnotic power, but admitted he had realised that only a strong leader could save this small community from the depths.

"You know, Inspector, I believe that," he went on earnestly. "The doctor has a never-ending library of stories; it really is a library. We listen to him telling stories, for so long as he will, such as Steinbeck's *Grapes of Wrath* and

Buchan's *Thirty-Nine Steps*. He's like Scheherazade who saved her life by telling the tales of the Arabian Nights, and if you close your eyes and just listen, you can almost live the stories. He has saved our lives, because even Riddell came to understand that these caverns hold something worse than perpetual darkness."

"And yet there are fights like that we witnessed today," Bony interposed.

"Oh, yes. Doctor Havant does nothing to stop them. He says the steam must escape through a safety valve; that the bursts of violence are the valve. These oppressive caverns have subjugated what virility we had; they do not exactly encourage the upshoot of the sexual urge. We are sane enough to realise that the first to attack the woman could be killed by the others.

"Igor Mitski died because of her. He was never any more than polite and friendly, but she teased him, and the others knew it. I've seen her encourage Mark, and even Riddell's ape-like advances. She invites murder—not her own, of course. I think she aims to have us kill one another until the best man wins. Meanwhile, she believes she has full control of us all, including you."

"What has she said about her own case?" asked Bony, and Maddoch's face expressed disgust.

"Said she killed her husband because she was sick of him and his lies, yet boasts how she put it over the jury, the press and the public; boasts how good an actress she is. You don't believe, really believe, I killed Mitski, do you?"

Bony turned to gaze steadily at Clifford Maddoch. To become the manager of a branch of an important wool firm is not an executive height to which a weak character can climb, and he tried to see Maddoch as he must have been before the final straw was laid upon his back. Mentally he would have been dynamic. He would have been expert on the many classes of wool, a man whose judgment was sound, and whose decisions were quick and accurate.

Once he had arrived at the moment of decision that no longer could he suffer his wife's nagging voice, he would immediately begin to plan how to remove it. And now— the once important executive, pleading to be believed he hadn't killed again. The yellow light revealed the large eyes, the colourless complexion, the trembling mouth of a man shocked by mental torture, racked by disgrace and punishment, and exposed to human violence and depravity. Execution would have been merciful.

"I shall answer that question if you promise not even to hint of it to the others" he said, and was troubled by the eagerness with which Maddoch assented. "Unless you have made a pair of stilts, Clifford, you couldn't have killed Igor Mitski."

Maddoch sighed audibly. "Thank you indeed, Inspector."

"Then let us be allies, Maddoch. I need an ally. You will understand that my position isn't, shall we say, normal, in relation to all of you. I need support, discreetly given, in things I must do and say; a secret ally who would keep me up to date on an intrigue hostile to me. How does this appeal to you?"

"You may count on me."

"Then I shall rely on you. Tell me, what d'you think of Doctor Havant?"

"A brilliant mind somewhere or other out of gear. I say that because I don't think he is unbalanced, just kind of out of gear. Maybe that applies to us all, yourself excepted. Life here is unnatural, and especially so for the doctor. Prison, Inspector, by comparison was heaven."

"I can believe that, Maddoch."

"Down here we are unable to get away from each other. And worse, we are unable to get away from ourselves, excepting those precious times when Doctor Havant becomes our story-teller. Accustomed to mental distractions such as books, the stage and the cinema, the newspapers, modern man quickly degenerates if deprived of such escapism. That is a threat to us all."

"Yes, that is true," conceded Bony, and stood.

"Hullo, that dog has run off again. Busy, isn't she? Now you see her; now you don't."

Lucy was being petted when they entered the 'hall'. A cloud masked the sun and the interior light was dim, the domed ceiling invisible. Doctor Havant and Riddell were sitting on the rock ledge, separated by something about three feet wide, and were moving lumps of rock. On Bony crossing to them, he found that the lumps were pieces and the game was draughts, the board being marked on the rock base by scoring with a knife point.

Both players being gravely intent, Bony moved to sit with Mark Brennan who, a little too casually, slipped a roughly square shaving of rock under his right thigh. He had been doing something to the piece of rock with a table-knife which at Bony's approach he employed to chip tobacco. Bony sat beside him, his back to the rock wall.

"You remember Jim Ord, Inspector?" asked Brennan.

"Yes, I do. Why?"

"He was in Goulburn with me. Used to tell us he'd have got away with murderin' a Swede up near Milprinka if you hadn't took a hand."

"Ord was clever, Mark. He made only two mistakes. Did he tell you what he said after I had him arrested?"

"Yes; just like him, too. He told you he wasn't wingeing about it. Said that when a bloke breaks the law, he is gambling against the cops, and it's a fair go. He was proud of what you said, too. It was, 'Ord, you really extended me.'"

"I remember," Bony admitted. "He was a good sportsman, yet knocking a man down with a loaded bottle and then kicking him to death isn't sporting."

"Well, look at what Stassan did to Ord's little girl. I don't hold with that sort of thing. Stassan got it just where he deserved it most."

"D'you really think, Mark, that the best way to get even is to kill?" asked Bony.

"With a bloke like Stassan, too right I do. And so do most of the other blokes in Goulburn. Queers and pimps and rapists ought to be hanged automatically, and when Ord booted Stassan to hell, he oughta got a knighthood. Thank Kelly we haven't a Stassan here with us. He wouldn't last long."

"Would you place Igor Mitski in that class?"

"No, Inspector. He just slapped the kid down a bit too hard, that's all. You know, sometimes you got to give a bit of licence. There's Mitski king-hit and belted around Europe. He's a musician and a top singer, and what happens when he comes to Australia? Stuck away out west, teaching a stupid brat brought up to the idea that she's the squatter's daughter, and the rest of the world is scum. I don't blame Mitski for slappin' her down. It was just his bad luck he larrupped her too hard. What's to do about him now?"

"The circumstances being what they are, the body will have to be disposed of without the usual legal formalities."

"Any idea who crashed him?"

"Not yet, but I shall, Mark."

"I know. We all know that when you start you keep on your feet. One of us killed Mitski, and he must know you will get him, sooner or later. His only hope is to do you in before you cotton on to him." Brennan smiled, and that he could smile was a revelation. "If he bumped you before we got out of here, before we got back to home and glory, I'd be really vicious for him."

"Have you any ideas on who killed Mitski?"

Brennan shook his head.

"Have you any ideas on why he was killed?"

"Yes."

"Well?"

"Against Institute rules to help the cops."

"Institute rules?"

"Yes, Institute rules, Inspector. The Institute of Released Murderers. You know, your Fellowship, remember? Here, this is your certificate."

From beneath his leg Mark Brennan produced the thin slab of limestock rock. He had scored plainly with the knife:

D. I. N. Bonaparte,
F.R.M.I.

From the stone Bony's eyes rose to meet those of the man who murdered twice within thirty seconds.

"Thanks, Mark, I shall treasure this unique scroll."

Chapter Fourteen

THE FEMALE JONAH

THE cloud passed from the westering sun, and swiftly the hall was transmuted to a place of warm colour. This effect was notable, even on Dr. Havant's chalky face, and strengthened Bony's first impression of him. He was sitting easily on the rock ledge, studying the draught board, and Bony could not make up his mind whether the doctor was intentionally encouraging Riddell, or was actually placed in a quandary by a man of greatly inferior intellect.

Having pocketed his 'scroll', he rose to his feet and crossed the chamber to become a spectator of the game. Riddell looked up, his small eyes illumined by triumph. The doctor continued to study the board, made once as though to move a man, hesitated, then did move it. Whereupon, Riddell countered, placing the doctor in a position from which there was no escape.

"Congratulations, Joe," Havant said, sliding his long body off the ledge. "Well, Inspector, how have you been getting along with Maddoch?"

"I've now a mental picture of these caverns and connecting passages, Doctor. The problem of who killed Mitski is similar to draughts, and a game I shall win. Meanwhile, there is the disposal of Mitski's body to be attended to."

"Agreed. What do you suggest?"

"I assume burial is out of the question."

"In earth, yes. There is only the one place for the body,

107

and that is down the crack where Fiddler fell. Shall I have it taken there?"

"Yes, and thank you, Doctor."

Havant regarded Riddell. He called for Jenks, and Jenks came from the alcove which served as the kitchen. In the same calm and formal manner, Dr. Havant said:

"I want you two fellows to take the body of our departed friend to Fiddler's Leap, and inter it."

Riddell's wide mouth tightened. Jenks' square face registered no emotion, but he said:

"Remember what Mitski told us happened when Art Fiddler fell down there?"

"Yes, Ted, I remember what he said about it," replied the doctor. "Subsequently there was the noise of a drain partially choked. Perhaps you could bring your majestic brain to bear on this matter, and suggest an alternative . . . cemetery."

The majestic brain tried to oblige, and failed.

"All right, then. Come on, Joe," assented Jenks.

"You might assist them, Mark, and you, Clifford, with lights," urged Dr. Havant.

Brennan went to the kitchen for the lamps, and they heard Myra Thomas say:

"What we call dinner, Mark, will be ready in half an hour. If you men want me to go on with the cooking, you'll be back for it."

"Okay, Myra," Brennan said. "If we ever get out of here, you won't have to do any more cooking."

"So you told me before, Mark." The voice was clear but low-pitched. They heard the soft laugh, the gentle tinkle of a pan. "Get going, Mark. The watch dogs are not far away."

The breath hissed from Riddell. Jenks chuckled. Maddoch said: "That's what I meant, Inspector."

The gorilla flashed about and punched the little man's chest, and Maddoch was spun and sent staggering, fighting for air. The voices and the words had triggered Riddell. It was as though a spark had jumped from the kitchen stove to a pan of gunpowder, and that when Riddell blew up, the explosion also ignited Jenks.

Jenks slid backwards to the wall to start his run, and Riddell, oblivious of Dr. Havant's shouted order, sprang towards Bony. Jenks didn't make his run. Havant did not repeat his order. Mark Brennan stood in the entrance to the annexe and little Maddoch fought to conquer his laboured breathing. They saw Bony side-step the charging gorilla, saw Bony flash in behind and slide his arms up under the big man's arm-pits, his hands lock behind Riddell's neck.

The indirect light from above fell upon Riddell's contorted face, and they saw the expression of Riddell's eyes change from fury to agony. They watched Riddell's wide mouth open to scream, and knew that he was too paralysed to scream. Uninhibited, accustomed to violence, yet Riddell's face revealed that he was enduring indescribable pain indefinitely prolonged. They watched Bony's thumbs working about the base of Riddell's skull, and even they were shocked.

Myra Thomas came to join them, and on seeing Riddell's face, her violet eyes opened wide, and her mouth curved into a smile as she said:

"You don't seem to be enjoying yourself, Joe."

Bony stood back from the huge body, and like a tree wrenched from its roots by a gale, Riddell fell stiffly sideways to the floor, where he lay on his back, his mouth opening and closing until relief came and he was able to scream.

The scream faded into sobs of anguish, and the girl's soft laughter.

"Go to your kitchen," Bony said.

Myra Thomas would have defied him had she not been caught by blue-ice eyes which grew and grew until she could see nothing else. She had resisted Havant's hypnotic eyes, but these were different, terrifying, magnetic and challenging. When she was freed, she ran to obey.

"Riddell! Get up!" commanded Bony, and Riddell groaned, turned over, humped and lurched to his feet. With legs splayed wide, he swayed drunkenly, eyes bloodshot, mouth but a sagging travesty.

"That is an aborigine hold, and many persons would pay much to learn its secret. I don't like applying it, Riddell, and I don't want to apply it to you again. And you others, pay attention. I command here. I hope to escort you from this place to civilisation, and therefore, you are not going to behave like wild animals. You will obey without question, and you will perform the tasks I set you. Convey that body to the place named and dispose of it."

Their shuffling faded into the tunnel-like passage. Maddoch crawled to Bony's camel gear and retched. Havant went to him. Bony entered the kitchen.

"Mrs. Thomas," he began softly. "I have had to deal with women exactly like you before. Doctor Havant will have a scientific term for your behaviour. You have a single-track ambition, but not here. Under normal conditions female coquetry is socially accepted. These are not normal circumstances, as you are fully aware. You will thus conduct yourself with rigid discretion."

Her dark eyes held only admiration as he reprimanded her. Her expression was subdued but her eyes defeated him. Her voice came softly on a note of seriousness.

"I can be the soul of discretion, Inspector. Anything I can do to help, just tell me. And I hope you will loosen up and call me 'Myra'."

"Where were you when Igor Mitski cried out?"

"Here, attending to the breakfast coffee. When I heard him, I knew he was in trouble, and I ran along the passage and found the others already there."

"The others. . . . Was Brennan there?"

"I think so, but I could be wrong. You see, I was upset by seeing Mitski lying in a pool of blood."

"You were playing him against the others?"

"What do you mean?"

"I repeat," Bony said icily. "Were you playing Mitski against the others?"

"I still don't understand what you mean, Inspector."

"I believe you do, but I'll put it another way. Were you arousing the men by encouraging Mitski, as you roused the others by play-acting with Mark Brennan here in this kitchen?"

The girl's eyes flamed scornfully.

"Do you actually believe I would encourage advances from murderers?"

"Yes. They are men." He indicated an empty box for her to be seated. "I shall keep to Igor Mitski, as you will, even if we do so for an hour, a day and a night. Mitski was a pointer, as Mark Brennan just now was a pointer, to your ambition, your attitude towards men, your reactions to this position in which you now find yourself. You are not unintelligent, and must know that in all hell there is no more violent loathing than that in the heart of a man made to appear a fool to himself. Did you permit Igor Mitski any intimacy, or just play-act with him?"

"To me Mitski was a musician, a singer, that's all," she declared, her voice now low and vibrant. "When I was tossed into this warren, it was like being one hen in a yard of roosters. You wouldn't know about that, but I haven't lost any feathers yet. I was brought up the hard way, and I got somewhere only by using the gifts I was born with. You men, you make me tired. Clever thinkers, protectors! I use my brain, and I have plenty to spare if you need it."

Was she being honest? Bony doubted it.

She went on more calmly:

"Mitski was gentle and thoroughly decent. He was like Cliff Maddoch, a dreamer, the kind of man a girl dreams about when she's seventeen, but when she's twenty, her man has to be the strong, determined type, the sort she has to fight off to save her virginity. Film stuff.

"When I was dumped here, it was Doc Havant who kept the roosters away, and it was Mitski who helped him carry me into the other annexe and nurse me out of the dirty drug I'd been given. I couldn't play favourites and so what could I do but be nice to Brennan and Riddell and the rest?"

Plausible! Reasoned! Genuine or fake? Did she believe what she said? Or was she blinded by vanity?

"I'll tell you what would have happened if you hadn't come," she went on. "The man who murdered Mitski planned to murder the others so he'd be the only rooster in the pen. In my opinion Riddell is that man. Riddell was quick in accusing Maddoch. And it was the kind of plan Riddell would think of. Which is why I was glad to see you giving that ape a little something to think about besides me."

"Then you believe that my coming alters the situation?"

"It couldn't possibly make it worse. Or could it?"

"Then will you please adopt an attitude of watchful coldness to everyone—especially me?"

"Certainly, Inspector—to the others."

"You know the story of Jonah—how the sailors tossed him to the whale because his presence aboard the ship was disastrous? You could find yourself situated as Jonah was, with no possibility of the whale being in Fiddler's Leap. Think about that."

She jerked her head swiftly to toss her hair from her face and, as he was about to leave, she stood to stir the large pot on the stove. In the doorless arch between the small and the large caverns, he turned to watch her. She must have felt his gaze for she looked over a shoulder at him and smiled, causing him to think that perhaps a dose of the medicine he had given Riddell might be effective.

Clifford Maddoch he found recovered, although the chest was painful, and Dr. Havant suavely promised banishment of pain by morning. They three took towels and soap to the Jeweller's Shop, where they washed and brought oil-drum buckets filled with water for the kitchen. The burial party returned, saying nothing, and they went off with towels also.

The cook served a substantial meal of Irish stew well seasoned with onions and potatoes, and it was Jenks who assisted Maddoch to wash the utensils. That done, the day above had departed, and Myra Thomas invited Havant to tell them a story.

"Yes, if you would all like me to," assented the doctor. "Last night I finished Jack London's *Burning Daylight*. In honour of the coming of our latest member, I shall tell you the story of *The Mystery of Swordfish Reef*, which I read several years ago, and is the record of one of Inspector Bonaparte's murder investigations. Agreed?"

"Unanimously."

Bony settled himself against Curley's pack-saddle, a well-fed Lucy sleeping beside him. The two lamps, placed on the floor in the centre of the chamber, revealed the doctor sitting, Eastern fashion, on a folded blanket, his back resting against the rock ledge, and the others in various attitudes. The doctor began the tale, and Bony was astonished by the

manner of the telling, which was as though Havant were
reading from a book. His listeners were so engrossed they
did not notice Lucy when, an hour later, she left Bony and
trotted off behind Brennan, to enter the kitchen. Perhaps
ten minutes after that—it might have been longer—she
barked at the company raptly listening to the story-teller,
and when the doctor ceased speaking, and the company
looked to see the dog bark from the edge of the opening
above, they were silent for a full pregnant minute. Then
Mark Brennan voiced the thought in all minds.

"If that dog can get out up there, so can we."

Chapter Fifteen

MITSKI OR GANBA

SOME time during the night, meaning the night above ground, Ganba roused Bony from well earned slumber. From the very intestines of the earth moved Ganba, creating sounds to fly along passages, through cracks, and echo from rock to rock. Sometimes one could hear Ganba slithering along a passage, being pinched by an overhang, then racing in freedom to an exit from which he could ensnare a blackfellow.

Bony had been sleeping on the floor of the main cavern, and within feet of the annexe where the men were sleeping. On being wakened by Ganba, he rolled a cigarette without bothering to ignite the hurricane lamp, and Lucy, obviously nervous, nuzzled against him.

Comforting her, he wondered if the dead Mitski was usurping Ganba's role. Mitski had said that after Arthur Fiddler fell to his death in the underground river, there arose direful sounds, suggestive of a great beast, replete and belching. When utterly alone, he had had the courage to trace the source of the sound to the split in the earth which had taken his companion, and he had reached the conclusion that the body was blocking the river, or partially so, like a choir boy's chewing-gum in the pipe of an organ.

In the men's sleeping quarters someone struck a match and lit a lamp, and Dr. Havant said:

"It's all right, Clifford. Only poor Mitski complaining of the manner of his burial."

"Wish he'd quit, then," Jenks grumbled. "He oughta know we don't have soft ground down here."

Nothing further was said, and soon the light was extinguished. The rumblings and the moanings died away, and Bony composed himself to sleep. When awakened by a further session of Ganba's peregrinations, he felt that he need sleep no longer, and for the second time made a cigarette.

A lamp was lit in the men's quarters, and then Jenks appeared with it, and stood looking down at him.

"Ruddy racket," he said. "Hope it don't go on for a month."

Without invitation, he squatted at the foot of Bony's blankets and bit hard into a plug of tobacco. With the casualness of the Australians down through decades, he asked:

"How you doing, Inspector?"

"Reasonably well, despite a mind crowded with questions," replied Bony. "A question I'd like answered now is, what have you people tried by way of escape?"

"Oh, that!" exclaimed the sailor indifferently. "Well, we got the notion of putting on a circus act. Doc worked out the height of the hole in the hall roof. The idea was for Joe to stand under it, and Mark to climb up and stand on his shoulders. Then for me to climb up them two and stand on Mark's shoulders, and Maddoch to shin up me and stand on mine. Doc reckoned that ought to get Maddoch high enough to grip the edge of the hole and haul himself out. We was gonna make a rope out of the blankets, and Cliff was to take one end up with him, find a place up top to tie it to, and the rest would be Jack and the Beanstalk."

"A good idea," agreed Bony.

"Yes, a beaut. But it didn't work out. We done a lot of practising, but still couldn't make a go of it. Mark managed to stand on Joe, but neither me or Cliff could get up to stand on Mark, because Joe wobbled too much. Gave it away after some of us got hurt."

"What about a blanket rope across Fiddler's Leap?" pressed Bony. "Ever try that way?"

"Thought about it, but no one was game to take the jump to the other side, and there's not much on the other side we could chuck a noose to bite on. Oh, we done some nutting out, Inspector. I thought I'd try and dig me way out. Went in for a yard or two, but the rock's too hard and they stopped me wearing out more knives. But there is a way out, ain't there? Must be. This here dog found it."

"Yes, she found it," agreed Bony.

"It don't matter how small it is, Inspector. If that dog got out, we can. Anyway, she got out, that's for sure."

"You still say you couldn't have missed an outlet?"

"Can't see how we could," asserted Jenks. "We've put in hours an' days crawling around on hands and knees, and poking our noses into bits of holes and cracks and what nots. Me or Mark have jockeyed on Joe's shoulders so's we could poke about the walls high as possible. Those bastards who put us down here musta made sure there's no getting out once you're in."

"There's the blow-hole, Jenks. If you are agreeable we'll look at that now."

"Suits me. Had enough sleep, anyhow."

Jenks led with the lamp, and when they entered the main passage a new day was indicated by the light in the distant hall. The passage off the main one twisted tortuously, was very narrow, and at some places barely high enough to give them movement. Then it widened and became higher, and the noise of the blow-hole ahead was loud and persistent.

"Sounds sort of different this morning," the sailor said, forging ahead. "She's always whined like a pup. Now she's moanin' like wind in the riggin'. Jeez! I'd give me soul to be at sea instead of down here in this stinkin' rat-hole."

The passage became small and they were forced to crawl, as though in a drain. Here the draught was distinctly strong, and the noise beyond a low and continuous roar. Ten or eleven feet of crawling brought them into a small chamber filled with pandemonium and wind, which caused the light to falter. At the far side of the chamber was an alcove without floor or ceiling. From below came the air spout, so powerful that it continued upward through the main roof. The air-flow within the alcove was like a metal bar against Bony's hand slowly thrust forward to meet it, and he could now understand how the girl's scarf had been drawn into the air spout and poised above the ground. There was certainly no exit here for Lucy.

He crawled back to the passage, tested the draught entering the hole, and decided that the girl need not have been near the air spout when the scarf was whisked away. Here it was possible to talk, and Brennan had said that he and the girl had come to talk.

"Old Doc Havant says the air pressure is caused by water banking up somewhere below. That right?" Jenks asked.

"Yes. Has it stopped since you have been here?"

"No. Sound alters a bit now and then. Knew an engineer one time. Clever bloke. If he was here and had the doings he'd make that spout work a generator to give us electric light. Say, wasn't that dog with us a minute ago?"

"Gone calling on the cook, perhaps."

"We'll be in on that, Inspector. I can smell coffee."

They found Riddell standing at the entrance to the kitchen and talking to Myra Thomas. He was unshaven and wore only trousers, his beefy torso clothed with hair. He drew aside when he saw them, and the girl who did not see them said:

"But, Joe, you know perfectly well that a woman needs a friend in a place like this."

"We got early visitors," Riddell said loudly. "Where you two been?"

"Workin', of course," snarled Jenks. "The dog here?"

"Yair, round about. Why?" demanded Riddell.

"Good morning, Myra." Bony greeted her as he entered the annexe which seemed to be filled with the stove and the girl standing beside it. "That coffee smells better than good."

"Been brewing for hours," she told him, filling two pannikins. "I couldn't sleep for that beastly row going on. You did, I suppose. You'd always do the right thing at the right time, Inspector."

Her black hair was combed to reveal her ears, and in this light her eyes appeared to be indigo blue. It was a pity, but undoubtedly necessary, that the male clothes she wore were ill-fitting, and neuterised her body.

"It's mere caution to look for the step before you raise your foot," he said without smiling. "My thanks for the coffee."

He withdrew to the hall, where he sat on his pack-saddle chair and appreciatively sipped the steaming coffee. Dr. Havant appeared, and after him came Maddoch, then Brennan who smiled at Bony and complimented him on following his nose.

"The first coffee and the first cigarette!" sighed Havant, who was exactly as he had been before going to bed. "What a night! That ghastly noise is beginning again."

"It frays my nerves," complained Maddoch, and Riddell sneeringly jibed:

"Why shouldn't it? Chucking Mitski down there sort of

119

blocked the drain. Now the poor devil is hollering for help. He's feelin' cold and all washed over, like. You'd be, too, you bloody fox, if someone bashed you with a rock and chucked you down the crack."

"That will be all from you, Joe," commanded Dr. Havant.

"Well, he did . . ."

"Control yourself, Joe. It's too early in the day to surrender to nervous reaction. We have work to do."

"Work! What's that?" sneered Riddell.

"Continuous use of the muscles which none of us have employed for a very long time, save Inspector Bonaparte. The dog! Has she been seen this morning?"

"She's here with me," called the girl from the kitchen. "We females have to guard each other. The breakfast menu is porridge and the usual tinned muck that our country also expects England to eat. It's all yours when you're ready."

There was a general exodus, and Bony followed with towel and soap, and the thought that he must soon shave or he'd be an ape, like Riddell.

Down in the Jeweller's Shop, its gems scintillating in the light of two lamps, the noise of Ganba was decidedly raucous, coming as it did along the passage from Fiddler's Leap. Before washing, Bony determined to prospect and, taking one of the lamps, he proceeded to negotiate what was little better than a rabbit's warren.

On stepping from the passage to the ledge at the great crevice, Bony sensed a change. The light percolating to the far ledge was as he had last seen it, but the distant rush of water had ceased. The level of the water was within a foot of the ledge, when it had been so far down that to drop a stone meant counting seven before hearing the impact.

The light fell upon the surface, to which now and then rose a large bubble of air, filled with sound not unlike that produced by an under-water swimmer. The released sound, exploding into the narrow confines of this rock chamber, blasted the ears with sledge-hammer rhythm.

Horror born of the theory evolved by the man whose body had been thrown into this noisome cavity subdued one part of Bony's being, and threatened the other. One part of his mind saw Ganba lurking in that wide ribbon of black water, and felt Ganba's breathing against his scalp. The other part of his mind registered the fact that within hours the water had risen almost to the ledge, and that, should it continue to rise, it would inevitably flood all these caverns and passages. And appalled by the threat of such catastrophe, he was driven back to the Jeweller's Shop by the pursuing voice of Ganba.

He remained at the stream only long enough to wash and comb his hair, and on again entering the hall, where he found the others at breakfast, he was master of himself, fury at an inherited phobia keeping him silent.

Dr. Havant enquired if the dog had followed him.

"She disappeared again, Inspector. We had forgotten to watch her. You are sure she did not go with you to Fiddler's Leap?"

"Quite, Doctor. Had she followed me, she would have gone no farther in face of the noise coming up from the crevice! We must work seriously to locate her outlet to the top. By restricting the area, we can narrow our search. Brennan and I will block with rubble the passage from the Jeweller's Shop to the crevice, and you others can block the passage to the blow-hole. If the way out is beyond one of those two barriers, Lucy will soon let us know when she's blocked. Myra can stay here and watch for her return."

While he and Brennan were blocking the passage with boulders to fit, so that the small dog could not get through, Bony felt himself unduly crowded. He had not informed the others of the danger he foresaw if the water continued to rise, lest panic should destroy effort. He was anxious to learn the escape route of the dog, anxious that the others should not know of it until they were fully prepared for what waited for them on the Nullarbor Plain. If without such preparation they gained freedom, the result would be more devastating to morale than panic at the threat of rising water. He said to Brennan:

"Did Mitski ever say how long these noises continued after Fiddler fell?"

"Didn't really know," replied Brennan, grunting as he rolled a boulder. "Like us, since Myra broke her watch, Mitski didn't have the time with him. He did say he guessed the racket went on for about twenty-four hours."

The noises ceased for approximately two hours when Bony judged it to be mid-day, and began again when they were eating what Dr. Havant called luncheon. Each glanced nervously at the others, and Bony said loudly to make himself heard:

"It's like a lot of drowning men, isn't it?"

"Please, Inspector!" pleaded Clifford Maddoch.

A minute later, Bony said, with a realistic shiver:

"I wonder if Mitski is struggling to come back to accuse his murderer."

"Cawl!" shouted Jenks. "Cut it out, Inspector. Gives me the willies."

And Maddoch screamed: "Yes, yes, cut it out. It's gruesome."

Maddoch stopped his ears with his fingers. Havant regarded everyone in turn, a faint derisive smile on his chalk-white face. Brennan's eyes were closed tightly, and Riddell sat hunched, still and waiting. In the archway to the kitchen the girl stood tautly, as though expecting Mitski to appear among them.

The rumbling, the moans, the gulping, stopped abruptly. The ensuing silence was even more harrowing. Then came one long loud crash and another silence. From the silence came Bony's voice:

"Sounds like Mitski pushing down the wall Brennan and I built. He could be coming from the Jeweller's Shop."

Maddoch moaned and shivered. The others made no sound whatsoever, sitting like men whose breath would never again be released.

Then pandemonium engulfed them. Their ears were bombarded. The rock on which they sat shuddered. From nowhere the dog raced upon Bony and buried her head in his lap. Maddoch seized the canvas tablecloth and wrapped it about his head.

Chapter Sixteen

BONY ADDRESSES THE R.M.I.

SOMEWHAT ruefully this time Bony sat back and watched the thaw of icy fear. Brennan's eyes moved as though by great effort. Riddell wetted his upper lip with the tip of his tongue, his eyes closed, one hand beginning to unclench. Jenks fumbled in his pocket for tobacco, and the girl moved her gaze from one to the other as though she had never before seen them. Dr. Havant appeared the least affected; he was still smiling as though at a joke none would understand.

Bony waited. His contribution to the build-up of Igor Mitski's return had not borne fruit. Mitski's murderer had not broken, and only Clifford Maddoch had almost reached breaking point.

Myra Thomas's next act was unexpectedly normal. She came forward and proceeded to gather the eating utensils scattered when Maddoch snatched up the 'tablecloth'. Tin plate meeting tin pannikin was a familiar sound, and this brought the men back to a degree of animation.

Maddoch removed the canvas cloth and looked stupidly about. Terror on his face was like a waxen mask which the sun of silence began swiftly to melt. His lungs expanded to take in air, and expelled the long deep breath. Jenks said:

"How did you like it, Cliff?"

"It was. . . . My wife was like that . . . between her

fits . . . as she was dying. I couldn't stand it . . . again.
Will it come again? Will it?"

Dr. Havant chuckled. He addressed Bony.

"Although the stage props were magnificent, Inspector,
the resurrection of our departed friend was too over-
whelming—which is to be regretted. It leaves our double
certificated murderer still hidden."

"My compliments on your acute perception," Bony
said, coldly. "Meanwhile, the problem of escape is now
paramount."

"Gettin' out's the main thing, and that ruddy dog knows
how," Riddell said importantly. "Why crawl about getting
backache and neckache when all we need do is loll around
and eye the dog. She won't stop running in and out 'cos we
happen to be watching her."

Jenks, the only one who had made determined efforts to
break out, suggested that the dog should be tied to someone.

"We must remember," Bony told them, "that Lucy isn't
a town dog, even though she is a United Nations. At least
one of her ancestors was a pure bred dingo.

"Many of these bush-bred dogs are close to pure dingo,
and, aware that their first litter was destroyed, will hide
their pups so cleverly that they never appear until she
permits them. You won't locate the pups by tying a string
from their collar to your ankle, or be led to them, if the dog
has the faintest suspicion you are watching her. You must
watch her without her knowing it, and that is not easy. You
must not make a fuss of her more than usual. To sum up.
If you rush this dog she'll stay put and laugh at you."

"The barrier idea is best," Havant said. "Let us extend it.
If she gets out this evening we shall know she didn't go by
way of the blow-hole passage or beyond the Jeweller's Shop.
We shall then station ourselves at various points to await
her return—waiting up for the errant daughter."

"Lot of common in that," contributed Jenks. "She's got to give herself away some time, the sooner the better. I've had this ruddy joint, and there's times when I reckon I can't stand no more of it."

"It won't be much longer, Jenks," Havant said, confidently, as the tough ex-sailor seemed about to break down. "Now isn't the time to abandon hope, but to permit it to revitalise our flagging spirits. As you have just mentioned, the dog will show us a way out eventually. And then . . ."

"And then I'm gonna hunt the swine who put us down here," Jenks said with the solemnity of a Crusader taking the vow. "Once I get me hands on one of 'em I'll be like the Irish terrier I had. I'll never never let go. Was it the Gov'ment put us down here?"

"Certainly not," Bony replied. "Who was instrumental in placing you people down here, I don't know—yet."

"Got any notions who it might be, Inspector? You been full of questions. You answer some. Answer that one."

"Theorising is often useless," temporised Bony.

"Yair! But a bloke can have some satisfaction in thinkin' what he'll do to them who put him here."

"That's the idea, Ted," purred the girl. "Meanwhile you could fill the stove with kero, and fetch water. I've an urge to do some baking this afternoon."

"That stove wants more kero?" Jenks snarled, getting to his feet. "Damn it, it eats oil."

"Please yourself. You're the boss," she snapped. "No stove, no bread, nothing."

"Pity someone couldn't boss you, you slut," yelled Jenks, and Brennan came charging from the kitchen.

"That'll do! Stop it!" shouted Bony. They coagulated like drying blood, and their furious eyes were ensnared by his. "Sit down, all of you. D'you hear? Sit down." Jenks cringed, turned to sit on a blanket. Brennan smiled sneeringly, and obeyed. The girl turned to go back to her kitchen, and Bony lashed her. "You, too, Myra. Or didn't you hear me?"

Turning, she regarded him superciliously and continued on her way. Brennan said, grit in his drawling voice:

"Better sit down, Myra. Might be knocked down if you won't. Looks like 'beg pardons' are old-fashioned." She sat, and Brennan continued to watch her. "I'll make you a cigarette," he promised, but she ignored the offer.

"That's better," Bony told them. "I intend to explain several matters clearly so that you will understand what is ahead and how damn silly it is to brawl among yourselves.

"I believe I know where the dog found her way out. If I am correct, it might mean days, perhaps a month of labour enlarging the passage, and you must be sufficiently intelligent to know that where Lucy can go, Joe Riddell might not.

"But no matter when we escape, the hurdles are many and severe, and you must realise just how severe if you hope to live. The best way, the surest way, is for all of you to remain quietly here while I go back for help and transport. You will have to wait only three weeks. You will . . ."

"Nothing doing," snarled Riddell.

"Wait here!" shouted Jenks. "Not for a million. I'd be out and away in a flash."

"Not for me, Inspector. I don't like Mitski's Dead March," Brennan said. "What about you, Doc?"

"I am going to be sensible and hear what Bonaparte has to say," replied Havant. "And I would be obliged did you people remain silent and listen to what he wishes to say."

"You will not suffer that noise again," Bony assured them. "The plug in the drain at the bottom of Fiddler's Leap has been forced through and the waters released. That is one danger eliminated. Now listen attentively.

"When we gain our freedom we have to walk two hundred miles to the nearest homestead. We could cover twenty-five miles a day, the journey thus occupying eight days. That is, of course, if all were in training. Can any one of you honestly say he has ever walked twenty-five miles, or even fifteen miles in one day? Can any of you be utterly confident of walking fifteen miles every day for a week after being cooped in these caverns for years? Of course not. If one or more of you didn't crack within a week, I'd turn gangster.

"Still, we could assume that all of us can walk at least ten miles a day, so that our journey will take twenty days, say three weeks. We then have to provision ourselves for those three weeks, also arrange our own water supply, because it's possible that for days on end we won't find any.

"What you must understand is that it won't be any question of the survival of the fittest. If, after I have placed all the cards face up, you are still determined not to wait for transport, then you will obey my orders without further argument, because it is my duty to return all of you to civilisation, not only the fittest, leaving the weak to perish.

"You will also understand that I am the only one among you who can lead you across the Nullarbor Plain, and that if anything should prevent me, say a blow to the back of the head, all of you will wander in circles until you drop and die. I can assure you that to perish of hunger, and especially of thirst, is the worst death you can suffer."

Bony paused for comment. They watched him: were silent.

"There is a large number of people, who, because they happen to be born in Australia, believe they know everything about this Continent. They travel by car or bus to towns in the farming belts, or by bus and car on the highways spanning this Continent, even encircling it, and believe they can be told nothing. Doctors and university professors, sailors and old maids—they know everything about Australia. And I have no reason to believe you are not of that vast number of know-alls.

"Since I informed you that you are now at the northern extremity of the Nullarbor Plain, have you asked yourselves why you were brought here when there are many such caverns within a few miles of the railway, within stone-throw of the only tourist road following the southern extremity? No. You have been so occupied with your grievances, imagined and otherwise. Why were you brought here? Because if you ever did manage to get out, the Nullarbor Plain would claim you as surely as though you escaped into a forest of ravening tigers.

"In fact, if you determine to accompany me back to civilisation, you are going to be beset by worse than tigers. Fatigue will torment you. Your tortured imagination will create monsters to stalk you. And Fear will snap at your heels."

Bony paused for emphasis.

"Remember, I shall be with you. You won't lie down when you are tired, because I shall boot you to your feet. You won't moan about being utterly exhausted, because I shall energise you with a burning match under your nose. If you leave here with me, you will arrive with me, even if then you are gibbering idiots.

"You won't bluff me. The Plain won't bluff me. But the wild aborigines might, so that those who accompany me will walk much further than ten miles per day." With studied insolence he added: "I trust I make myself clear enough for your limited understanding."

Again he paused for comments, and again none were offered.

"When I set out to look for Myra Thomas, I had no

knowledge of the disappearance of you men, your failure to report in accordance with your release doubtless being attributed to defiance. I have been in this part of the country for three weeks, and did not once find any evidence of aborigines. I did admit to that possibility . . . of wild aborigines wandering this northern extremity of the Plain, but had no reason even to assume that there might be aborigines working for people who abducted released murderers, and who were instructed to await my arrival and capture me did I locate these caverns, and then add me to the members of the Institute.

"It is certain, if I accept the contacting of the aborigines before my arrival, which I do, that they will have contacted those white people who conveyed you here, and that the aborigines have been ordered to maintain watch over this part of the country, just in case I manage to escape and go back for assistance. Therefore, the wild aborigines represent the great obstacle confronting me as your leader.

"You think you know all about the aborigines, having seen them driving farm implements or trucks, their children going to school, and their women attending sewing classes. Perhaps you have seen them drinking milk shakes in town cafés, and even reading newspapers and books, and attending a cinema. Doubtless you have always regarded them as spineless nitwits, being infinitely below your own regal white-folk intelligence.

"You will not be amused when I tell you that the wild aborigine, in his own unfenced and unfarmed country, places you as little innocent, squawking ducklings, running around just waiting for your necks to be wrung. Can you see yourself, Doctor Havant, or you, Joseph Riddell, as a little duckling? I can.

"I do not assert that if we are captured by the wild aborigines we shall be massacred or we shall become the sport of savages. I state with utter conviction that if we are caught we shall be returned to these caverns and guarded well until another jail is found for us, or the exit has been sealed for ever. And I have no wish to remain here, for ever.

"If you have any sense left, you will remain here until I return with transport. I could do that within two weeks. My reputation is my guarantee that within three weeks you will be back with the crowds and the lights of your pet city. And what tales you will have to tell! What publicity, fame! Free food and drinks. The opportunity to make even enough money to muzzle the taxation bloodhounds.

"If you come with me, you cry with fatigue, you may moan with the pain of my boots, you may even die, but your body will arrive with me at the end of the journey you could have made in a comfortable car or aeroplane."

Chapter Seventeen

VISIONS OF FREEDOM

"TOUGH guy!" Riddell said, sneeringly.

"Quiet," commanded Dr. Havant with unusual severity.

"Sez you," persisted the hairy man.

"Riddell, look at me." Riddell was obstinate; Dr. Havant determined. Riddell visibly cringed. "I say, Riddell," repeated Havant. To Bony he continued.

"As you requested, we have listened attentively. What you have told us is the essence of common sense, and your picture of the Plain an undeniable endurance test. I agree that we must wait here for you to send relief. As a medical man I agree that we are not fit enough to undertake the journey."

"I'm not hanging around here," Jenks asserted. "Not for mine. I can walk the trip. I'm going with Bonaparte."

"Me, too," declared Brennan. "I'll be on my way from the toe line. If I can't walk two hundred miles, I'll go crawling on hands and knees. I want to feel the wind and the sun; the big black boys don't scare me."

They waited, waited as though for Riddell to cast his vote, but Riddell glared at them, was silent. Maddoch then said:

"If you, Doctor, decide to stay, I'll stay with you."

"Thank you, Clifford," Havant replied. "Riddell, I think you had better go."

"I'm goin', Doc. Don't worry."

"And so shall I," added the girl.

"No," advised Havant. "You must stay with Clifford and me."

"It would be too dull. You two together don't even add up to one real man." Her eyes mocked. Easter's assessment now proved right.. "All of you have given me only sensational radio material, enough to make real money, and I'm not missing out. I don't intend to be Daniel, left with two tame lions."

"You could be disaster, Myra, for the lions you would accompany," she was told, coolly. "The lions, as you now call us all, might not get through because of you, a woman, and therefore, a weak link."

"I'm as strong as any one of them, and no one will stop me from going with Inspector Bonaparte. Not even Bonaparte."

"Sez you," snarled Riddell, and she turned on him.

"Shut up, you repulsive gorilla," she shouted. "Shut up, you . . . you . . ."

"I second that," softly interposed Mark Brennan. "Myra, calm down. You're a lady, remember? You will do just what the Inspector decides. If he says you must stay here, you stay. Because, Myra, I won't let you spoil my chance of getting back to Pitt Street on a Saturday night. I'll bloody well choke you to death first. Get me, Myra?"

The violet eyes turned to Bony, who decided it would be wiser to have the woman under his own lash, for those who stayed would be in the position to betray those who went. He said:

"In Myra's favour is the fact that she has been here only a short while, and, physically, would be fitter than those who have been here for a year and more.

"Now, let us be clear. Doctor Havant stays, and Clifford thinks he ought to stay also. You others have elected to go with me. Mark Brennan, I like your spirit. I applaud your determination not to permit Myra, and others may be included, to ruin your chance of returning to civilisation. May I expect you to support all my decisions?"

"You may. Too ruddy right, you may."

"Then, our next step. Because the way out taken by the dog might be comparatively easy for us, I warn you that to escape into the open in broad daylight could well mean the smashing of all our hopes. There are those wild aborigines, with eyesight like eagles. From our present position we cannot know where they are, and thus they could be watching for us to emerge, waiting like dingoes for rabbits to bolt. To our great advantage is their fear of the Plain by night. So we work our way out by night. We emerge by night. Your journey to freedom and the bright lights begins by night. Now go to it. Look for Lucy's passage in the kitchen."

Bony was left, seated on Curley's pack-saddle and rolling a cigarette. Even Dr. Havant rushed to the kitchen. Bony was reminded of his three boys at home when, as reward, he had started them on a treasure hunt.

Havant had performed miracles under extraordinary circumstances. He had preserved their sanity, and in so doing had preserved human decency, under mind-destroying conditions.

They had obeyed simple sanitary rules and kept themselves reasonably clean, retained a form of civilised eating. They conformed to rough but invaluable community demands and, if occasionally they lost control, the loss was temporary and beneficial.

For twenty-five years he, Napoleon Bonaparte, had hunted murderers. He regarded murder as the most loathsome crime. He had viewed the bodies of the slain, and was nauseated by the public sympathy for murderers, and the cold indifference to the murdered. He believed there was but the one penalty for murder: an eye for an eye, the justice of the Bible, the justice of the aborigines.

Here were six murderers, and here was he who loathed murderers and hunted them relentlessly. Right now could he hate Clifford Maddoch? Or Mark Brennan? Even animal Joe Riddell? Havant was something of an enigma. The girl was a type he disliked, beyond the fact that she was a murderess.

When engaged on a man hunt, the murderer had been an impersonal thing, like a wild dog. This hunt for a lost woman, which had led to the discovery of a community of murderers, had become personal. They accepted him without rancour, even making him a Fellow of their absurd Released Murderer's Institute.

There was not among them a human tiger beyond reformation, save only, perhaps, that one who had killed Mitski. Imprisonment had imposed discipline and reliance on the officers. Time tended to heal animosity against the police responsible for their arrest and the judge responsible for the sentence. As Brennan had hinted, they had acquired loyalty to their fellows, and a kind of pride of the jail where they had served their sentence. It was something akin to the soldier who takes pride in his regiment, and is loyal to his comrades.

By welcoming Bony into their Institute, they were running true to form. The police had done a job of work, and the warders had performed another job. They and their opponents were in different trades unions, that was all.

He must beware of such reflections lest they should influence his approach to future man hunting. A lover of justice, he must recognise the danger of maudlin sentiment. The State—that easy front for diplomats, politicians, and appointed scoundrels—had defied and frustrated the courts of justice to gain personal kudos. The State was responsible for surrendering to mass hysteria, representing so many votes, and reducing the crime of murder to the level, of say, bigamy. His duty now was to do all possible to return these murderers to civilisation, when his official interest in them would end. With one exception.

They returned from the kitchen, wilting like cut flowers. "The hole is behind the rock at the back of the stove," Mark Brennan announced. "We can't move the rock; we'd need such things as crowbars and gelingnite. Looks like we're sunk."

Bony entered the kitchen. The stove had been moved to one side. A great boulder, or an upthrust of rock, had either fallen from the ceiling, or had been parted from the wall, creating a space of a little less than one foot. In this space, the dog had found the outlet at the foot of the wall.

"Take an atom bomb to shift that," jeered Riddell, and the girl said brightly:

"That all? We'll ask the aborigines to pass a few down."

"You can reach in, Inspector, and feel the hole in the wall about a foot up from the floor," Maddoch informed him.

"The dog," Bony ordered.

Lucy was brought. Bony on his knees pushed her forward, urging her to "Sick 'em! Sool-'em-up!"

Lucy required little persuasion. She disappeared. Silence enabled them to hear her muffled barking, and when no one followed her, she returned. Bony suggested that they try again to move the boulder.

He assisted. They heaved and hauled and pushed, grunting from the effort.

"Must be an upthrust, all right," he said. "Anyone done any mining?"

Jenks claimed to have worked on sinking wells in the New England district of New South Wales.

"We'll try an explosive charge, Jenks. Could you bore a hole in this rock for the charge? It will take time."

"With what?" Jenks asked.

"I have eight steel tent pegs and a small hammer used for driving in pegs and repairing dingo traps. I'll get them."

They followed him to his pack-bags, from which he produced the hammer and pegs, and Jenks examined the pegs with care.

"They're not steel, but good iron," he said. "But wait on, now. Where's the explosive?"

Bony produced two boxes, each containing fifty high power rifle cartridges.

"We extract the bullets. Cordite might do the trick," he pointed out.

"Yair, but what about detonators to set her off with?" persisted Jenks, and Bony explained that each cartridge had a percussion cap or detonator, and for fuse they would have to fashion a train of kerosened rags, light it, and run like hell.

"It mightn't work," he warned them. "We can but try."

"You're just tellin' us," agreed Riddell. "Let's give it a go, Ted."

"First, remove the stove," Bony advised. "Do it now, and Myra can get on with her baking. And grab that dog. She'll have to be tied up."

The indignant Lucy was attached to the riding saddle, and Bony sat beside her. He could hear the low thuds of the 'miners' at work, and watch Myra, who was absorbed with her cooking, obviously an avenue of escapism.

Havant came to sit beside Bony. The shaft of sunlight fell between them and the entrance of the main passage, and across the opening above passed woolly white clouds which Bony could only guess were southward bound.

"You are wise to elect to wait for relief, Doctor," he said, when it became apparent that Havant waited for him to speak. "I wish the others possessed as much wisdom. If we do manage to get out and away, you will not jeopardise our chances by making a rash move?"

"Of course not. That would react on me, Inspector. What are your difficulties? What can I do? You will find me anxious to co-operate."

"My main worry is those wild aborigines. As I said, they will not rove the Plain at night, being too fearful of Ganba. This place is but three miles from the northern desert country where they live and feel safe.

"If and when we can use the passage taken by the dog, we must on no account attempt to leave during daylight. It would be essential to be at least ten miles out on the Plain before the night passes, and we must trust to luck that our tracks won't be found and followed. Alone, I wouldn't have the slightest worry. With the others, and one a woman —you know their physical condition.

"Assuming we can prevent undue haste, even panic, those who wait must on no account use that passage. In fact, I shall ask you to block it. You could resist the temptation to use it, even at night, but do you think you could control Maddoch?"

"Yes. The woman, no. I shall be glad if she leaves with you."

"You are not an admirer?"

"I am not an admirer, Inspector. To me she is repellent. She has likened herself to a hen in a yard of roosters, a Daniel in the den of lions. Actually she isn't a hen, or a female Daniel. She is sexless without knowing it, but her husband knew it, and the knowledge was the basis of the animosity which led to his death.

"She has what is termed, in layman's language, a split mind, and I don't mean a split personality. One part of the mind worships Myra Thomas, and the other constantly defends a Myra Thomas who is fearful of men, of sex, and of the penetration by women of the vanity behind the façade. So take her with you and lose her, Inspector."

"She goes with us, Doctor. Now tell me, what is your opinion of Mark Brennan?"

"Brennan was, I think, the least affected by legal imprisonment, and subsequently by these caverns. He realises most clearly his dependence on you to get them through. A likeable fellow in many ways, but . . . the psychiatrist can cure the mind which once was healthy; he can do nothing for a mind deformed at birth. I was able to do a great deal for Mitski. I have been able to help Maddoch. Nothing can be done for Brennan. But you will find him an excellent first mate. Riddell is merely a body ruled by low intelligence. Jenks is slightly higher and, I have discovered, the hardest to understand. There is a lot of good in Jenks. As for Doctor Havant, well, you know about him. You found him sucked dry of the will to live. You will find. . . . Did you see that shadow?"

"Yes. There is someone up there."

Chapter Eighteen

THE SMELL OF FREEDOM

"STROLL normally to the kitchen and tell them to stop work on the rock. Ask Brennan to come to me—without haste."

Havant rose and crossed to the annexe. The girl went on with her cooking. Bony yawned deliberately, lit a cigarette and avoided glancing up at the opening in the roof.

"Sit down, Mark, I want to talk to you," he said when Brennan appeared. "I shall rely on you to assist me in maintaining some kind of discipline from now on. I have been telling the doctor that our greatest hurdle is the aborigines. If you look up casually you may see one, or his shadow. The shadow of a man will move faster than that of a cloud."

"Abo, all right, Inspector. One's looking down at us now."

"Be natural. Make a cigarette." On looking upward, there was then nothing to be seen other than the fading blue of the early evening sky. "Are you convinced, Mark?"

"Yes, of course. Why?"

Bony reiterated what he had told Dr. Havant.

"And so we break out of here precisely as though we were in Coulburn jail. Those aborigines are the warders, Mark. But we haven't a night watch to contend with, and therefore all our work must be done at night. I'm glad that fellow's appearance convinced you; you could help me to convince the others."

"Sure thing, I'll do that. I understand, too, that we could make a muck of things, and toss away a hell of a good chance. The others'll have to be drilled and bashed if they won't fall in. You'll find me on your side all the way. As I said, I'm going to get there, and I'm not standing for any back chat."

"Good! How's the boring going?"

"In about two inches. Think those abos heard the tapping?"

"They could have done, but if we don't persist they'll be baffled. Tell the others to come out here and relax, pretend they are bored, fed up, and all that. I may persuade Myra to brew a billy of tea."

As Brennan was leaving, Myra left her stove and stood before Bony. He stood also, inviting her to be seated with him on the pack-saddle.

"What's the conference about?" she asked, coolly.

"Aborigines. They're up top."

"How d'you know that?"

"I saw their shadows. Mark saw one fellow looking down at us."

"Oh! I thought you were plotting to leave me behind."

"I ought to have been doing just that, but I wasn't. You have a pair of walking shoes?"

"Don't be silly. All I had on was a gown over pyjamas and a pair of slippers, when I found a man waiting outside the lavatory on the train. He hit me instead of inviting me to dress. A lady doesn't expect that kind of treatment, you know."

"Two hundred miles is a long walk in bare feet."

"The men haven't any boots or shoes, Inspector. You're lucky."

"The men's feet are hardened. Yours are not. I am warning you that, should we escape, and should you refuse to wait with Havant and Maddoch, you may be abandoned."

"I would prefer even that to staying here a second longer than necessary. You don't know what it's like being a woman without a thing to wear."

"But I do know that you have much for which to be grateful to the doctor."

"Him!" she exclaimed, witheringly. "I wouldn't be left alone with him for a million pounds, even though he could get me out of what he'd get me into. Still, I don't know. A million . . ."

"What about making us all a cup of tea?"

"Tea! We're talking about falling in and out of sin and you ask for tea. I could adore a man with a sense of humour."

She spoke quietly, looking at Bony with unconcealed admiration, her eyes candid and open to her mind. And still Bony was unable to decide whether she was being herself or Mae West.

She made the tea, and presented each of them with a small cake she took from the oven. The doctor had schooled the men, and when he proposed a game of draughts, Riddell agreed. Bony invited Jenks to sit with him.

"Hard rock?" he asked.

"Worked harder . . . and softer. Went in about two inches so far with only one of the pegs. How far you think she oughta go?"

"Eleven or twelve inches," replied Bony. "What is your guess?"

" 'Bout that. Take a long time."

"That can't be avoided. Anyway, we dare not fire the charge till after midnight, to be on the safe side."

"You sure them blacks is up above?"

"Brennan saw one looking down. I saw their shadows. So did the doctor. They are up there, unquestionably, Jenks."

"Like to get me hands on one of them."

"A pleasure which would be short-lived."

"We takin' that tart with us, if we get out?"

"Should she wish to accompany us."

"Gonna to be a drag."

"Better for us all that she goes. If she remains she might do something foolish which would give away our escape to the abos."

"Then better dong her and chuck her into Fiddler's Leap." The suggestion was serious. It startled Bony, and he glanced sharply at the ex-sailor. A grin appeared to widen the greyish stubble on his chin. "I keep forgettin' you're a detective, Inspector."

"That could be dangerous, Jenks. We shall get through if we pull together, and if we don't panic."

Bony detailed to Jenks the kind of opposition they would meet, and, as with Brennan, he urged extreme caution. An hour later he seized the opportunity to talk with Riddell.

"Joe, you are the strongest man here," he concluded. "Much depends on you. We shall have to take water, most of which you will be called upon to carry. After the first two or three days' travel, speed won't be so urgent, but food and drink will be essential right to the last yard. If we were in a real jail and planning a breakout, you would do your part, and see to it that the rest did theirs. Now, wouldn't you?"

"You're tellin' me, Inspector. What you says goes, and I'll crash the bloke wot argues about that."

The colour faded from the faraway patch of sky and, eating dinner by lamp-light, they waited for the first star to appear above them. And when the star swung into the ragged patch, Bony permitted them to continue with the boring.

Instantly they became again like boys setting out on

adventure, working in relays, hammering the tent peg into the deepening hole having a diameter of little more than an inch. Dawn was promising another day when the hole was drilled sufficiently.

They packed cordite into the hole. The caps were packed in, and, grinning joyfully, the keeper of kerosene liberally drenched torn up cartons and rags to serve as the fuse. It was Riddell who suggested that Bony take the honour of applying the match.

In the hall they waited, Bony hoping that the dawn wind would blow the fumes of kerosene and burning material out over the Plain. The blast snapped against their ears, produced a cheer and a rush to the kitchen. The boulder lay split into three sections.

They dragged the slabs away. They fought each other to lie prone, and look into the small hole, but a little larger than that Lucy would need. The scrimmage thus early made Bony despair. When it was over, and they all had looked into the hole, he said coldly:

"May I now examine the result of the work on the boulder?"

"Yair, of course," responded Riddell, and Brennan had sufficient grace to be ashamed. He said: "You can see daylight, Inspector. But our chances don't look so good."

Through a funnel Bony could see a larger space beyond it. The funnel sloped upwards sharply, and was less than two feet long. The space beyond the funnel appeared to be a narrow passage rising but a fraction less sharply than did the funnel.

He ordered a lamp to be brought, and pushed it into the funnel to examine the rock surround. Then he saw faint lines of close cracks, and hope blossomed again.

"Jenks!" he called. "See those cracks?"

"Cracks, all right," agreed Jenks. "Could try 'em out and

might break through. Or another charge might shift some thing. Any cordite left?"

"A little."

"It's on again. Reach me that hammer and iron."

"Not now," Bony said. "No hammering until tonight. Here's the peg. Try levering here and there."

The peg was blunt, and Bony called for a fresh one, rolling aside to permit Jenks the room he required. He could hear the point of the peg feeling rock, and now and then Jenks grunted.

"Might shift something with about two taps of the hammer," Jenks said, and again was told to wait.

Bony sat up, to encounter the gaze of the circle of spectators.

"Go to the hall. Sing. Sing anything, but sing, and keep on singing. Beat time, mark time, to make a row. But keep it going."

With 'party' enthusiasm, tin plates were beaten and Myra Thomas began singing 'Long, Long Trail'. Bony was astonished by the quality of her voice, and soon other voices joined in.

"Go to it, Jenks," he said, presenting the sailor with the hammer.

Even thus close to the impact of the hammer, the sound was negligible. Bony could do nothing to help Jenks and the waiting gave him opportunity to plan the next move, could the opening be enlarged.

'Long Trail' became the 'Bells of St. Mary' and the 'Bells' changed to the chant of 'Three Blind Mice'.

"A bit's givin'," gasped Jenks. A move of position, the passing of a naked forearm across a bristly face, further effort. Then came a sound not of the hammer, a significant sound, and Jenks withdrew to examine the funnel by the light held by Bony.

"Might bring down a ton or two of the ruddy wall. I know. Get us a line I can fix to the peg and then we'll haul when standin' well away."

The released Murderers' Institute Singers were back on the 'Trail' when Bony crossed the hall to his gear. With hands and head he encouraged them to continue, and with greater vigour. Jenks found slight difficulty in attaching the line to the peg to give a degree of leverage. He grunted and swore, and grinned when they edged back towards the entrance of the hall. He spat on his hands, gripped the line, nodded to Bony who pressed behind him, and slowly they hauled.

They could feel the peg moving. Against the distant light they saw the shape of the funnel altering . . . to become static again. They tried again with a fresh peg, the first bent and useless. And then there came a low grinding sound, and abruptly the shape of the funnel altered again. The funnel had become a tunnel.

"Ahoy!" Jenks cried, and darted forward to the hole, now big enough to permit even Riddell to pass with comfort.

"Wait" shouted Bony, and Jenks looked back when on hands and knees he was about to crawl through the opening —backward and upward into the muzzle of an automatic. "Stand up, Jenks. If you don't obey, I'll certainly shoot. That's better. There will be no breaking out until dark tonight."

"Ruddy gun! You gotta a ruddy gun? Caw! I wasn't goin' to do no harm, Inspector."

"I thought you might, Jenks. In your excitement of course. Bring the gang."

They stood just within the entrance, to see Bony squatted on his heels before the ragged opening, the pistol in full view. He could see the elation in their eyes, their quivering mouths, their hands which trembled as though they held freedom, for now, at once. Before they could speak, he called Maddoch to him.

"I am trusting you, Maddoch," he said. "And if you fail me I'll shoot you like a rabbit. Go through the hole, follow the passage beyond, see where it leads. Go as far as possible, and stop before you reach the open, if there is an opening to the ground above. Clear?"

"Yes. You can trust me, Inspector."

The little man slid by into the hole. They heard the clink of rocks being moved to permit passage, and then only silence. Bony said:

"Brennan, come here." Brennan came forward and was told to stop at five feet from Bony. "I am trusting you, too, Mark. Remember what we spoke of about discipline?"

"Of course. What do I do?"

"I don't want to shoot anyone, Mark, but I am determined that our break-out shall be at the right time, in an orderly manner. I trust you to back me. The same applies to the rest of you. You have been warned repeatedly, and now I expect you to behave with reason and for the benefit of us all."

The initial surge of excitement threatening the bounds of control was subsiding, and resentment which had flamed in Jenks was dying. Silently they waited for the return of Maddoch.

Maddoch came to the broken wall, came through the opening fast. He was beaming with joy, his face transfigured. He reported to Bony:

"The passage goes on up and then slightly left. There's a long crack in the roof about two inches wide which provides the light. When I saw the end of the passage I thought I could go no further. But I could. There's a narrow slit on one side, and I could just squeeze through it into a sort of tunnel. It's just big enough for me to negotiate, but the sides and roof are all rubble so it can be made big enough for Joe. The other end of the tunnel comes out into a kind of shallow hole covered with saltbush."

Triumphantly he produced sprays of this miniature shrub, and they surrounded him, to touch the velvety succulent leaves. The girl held a leaf against her cheek, and to Bony came the thought that this was the woman, natural for once.

Maddoch clutched his arm, and he turned to look into appealing eyes and see the faintly trembling lips.

"I want to go, too, Inspector. I could smell the sunshine out there. I felt it on my hand when I slipped it outside, just for a moment. I must go with you. I couldn't stay now."

Chapter Nineteen

THE PLAIN WAITED

AT breakfast Bony felt that his fellow prisoners were less edgy than he had known them, and this he believed due to sound sleep and realisation that discipline was essential. Following the meal, he had slept in the hole enlarged by the explosion, so that none could pass him and break out to the Plain. Brennan had elected to stay in the hall with Havant to allay suspicion should the aborigines chance to come again, and Myra, saying that she had some rough sewing to do, had retired to her 'room'.

On waking, Bony found both the doctor and Brennan asleep, and from the angle of the sun-shaft judged the time to be about three o'clock. He proceeded to explore in Maddoch's steps, and checked the little man's report with satisfaction. An hour's work at one place only would clear the way for the massive Riddell.

He was brewing coffee when Myra appeared in the kitchen where the stove had been returned. She asked two questions.

"Would you make me a cigarette with your tobacco? Do we start tonight?"

She had evidently slept well. Her manner was cheerful and she was eager to co-operate. He told her they would leave early this coming night, completed a cigarette for her and poured the coffee.

"There is a deal of preparation to be done, Myra, and I

want you to bake as much bread as possible between now
and, say, seven o'clock. Give us a solid stew for dinner.
What possessions do you want to take?"

"Possessions! I haven't any excepting a broken comb,
my nail scissors and a small mirror. Is it going to be as hard
as you've made out?"

"Every bit—especially on our feet. I'll make shoes for
you which will help a little. I still urge you to remain."

"I am going, Inspector," she said, with sudden tightening
of her mouth. "I'll get through, for you won't find me
weaker than the men. I've too much to live for."

"Smelling headlines already?"

"It's like attar of roses."

"Then permit me the homely smell of lunch while I wake
the others."

They were gathered about the canvas cloth when Bony
outlined the preparations to be made, and now the only
rebel was Lucy, who sulked at being tethered to the camel
saddle. After the meal, he ordered all the lamps to be lit and
taken to the main cavern, where they could work unseen by
chance visitors above.

Having set aside a blanket for each traveller, he put Jenks
to work at tearing several blankets in strips, and Brennan to
fetch supplies of tinned meat, coffee and sugar, a bag of
flour and oddments, including matches and tobacco. One
of the water drums was filled by Riddell at the stream in the
Jeweller's Shop.

"Maddoch! Are you still determined to go?" Bony asked,
and Maddoch nodded, after glancing at Dr. Havant. The
doctor said he would wait with what patience he could
muster, and was not by any means dismayed by a period of
solitude.

Distributing the weight as evenly as possible, the five
blankets were rolled about the foodstuffs and oddments,

tied with strips of blanket and fitted with slings to carry the roll from the shoulder, *à la* sundowner's swag. In readiness, they were placed in the kitchen, and with them was put the water-drum and the rough harness Riddell was to wear to carry it. Bony did consider taking old Patsy's one-man tent, but decided against it.

"We are almost finished with our preparations. Nothing superfluous," he told them. "The last thing to be done is to fashion shoes with pieces of blankets. You see . . ."

"My feet are tough enough," Jenks interjected, and was supported by Riddell.

Tersely Bony told them of the precaution taken by an aborigine to prevent his tracks being followed—the gluing of masses of feathers to the feet with blood.

"The next best material is wool from the sheep's back. As we have neither feathers nor wool, we must use the blanket. And we have to be quite sure that our blanket shoes won't come off; they will be a little ungainly at first."

They made pads to fit the soles of their feet, and the pads were bound with strips of blanket which were wound up to the knees like puttees, Bony warning them that the low bush was tough.

"Looks like we're off to the South Pole," remarked Myra. "If only we had a camera! What sights for sore eyes we'd be on television. How do I look?"

Placing one hand on a hip, she danced across the uneven floor; Brennan chuckled, and Bony had to smile.

"On television, Myra, you'd knock 'em for sure. That patch on your bottom looks terrific." Brennan chortled, and Bony suddenly realised this Brennan was new to him. As was the girl. Even Maddoch had changed. His eyes were alive.

The sun-shaft gleamed redly on the wall of the circular

hall, when Bony asked Havant to accompany him that he might do certain work after the party had left. Taking Havant to the exit, he spoke softly.

"There, beyond that mask of bush, is what might give you rebirth. Can you deny yourself that chance?"

"Quite, Inspector."

"Then I must accept your decision. After we leave, will you block this exit tightly with rubble for several feet inward, to prevent its chance discovery."

"It will provide a task. I will do that."

"Record the days with a mark on rock," advised Bony. "Shall I insist that Maddoch remain with you?"

"No. But I think Maddoch should stay for his own good, if the conditions are as you have pictured them."

"I haven't exaggerated. With luck all should endure the physical strain. It is the mental angle which gives me no little concern. I believe that Maddoch will stand up to the mental stress as well as Jenks or Brennan, even the woman. However, I'll talk to Maddoch again."

They were silent for a space, when Bony said:

"What do you intend doing when you return to normal life?"

"Oh!" softly exclaimed Havant, as though the question surprised him. "I have a small grazing property in the southern Riverina. It's been managed for me during my absence, and I was to go there following my release. The authorities will, I assume, insist that I comply with the conditions set down by them."

"Perhaps the authorities will not insist," Bony said. "I shall leave nothing undone to convince them of your services to the unfortunates imprisoned here with you. Those conditions could be lifted."

"Could they? Then, I would settle somewhere in North Australia, under another name. I . . . er . . . am a little nervous of the publicity this affair will create. The abduction of Myra, especially, was too dramatic for her return not to arouse world interest. She is beginning to realise it, too."

"Every picket in a fence she'll make a winning post, Doctor. I shall see you again within three weeks, and I want you to regard me as a friend on whom you can call for all assistance you may need. That is, if you did not murder Igor Mitski. Did you?"

"No. I'll tell you why I did not. Excepting Maddoch, Mitski was the only cultured man here. Also I am no longer attracted to women physically, and the murder of Mitski was prompted by jealousy. Murder was inevitable. If Mitski hadn't been killed, another man would have been. If you hadn't come, others would have followed Mitski down Fiddler's Leap. The one thing which saved that woman from her own folly was the number of the lions in the den. Mitski's killer intended to reduce the number to one—himself."

"You could be correct, Doctor. Well, I must return to our final preparations for departure. The sun has set."

On entering the kitchen, they could hear laughter in the hall. Riddell had commandeered the hair clippers and was close-cropping his whiskers. Jenks was shaving, frowning with concentration, and Maddoch said that they were dressing for the theatre. But all were wearing the blanket boots, and there wasn't an aborigine in Australia who would fail to deduce the purpose of that footwear. Inwardly Bony groaned, for he had told them not to appear in the hall.

"You wouldn't have noticed an aborigine looking down at you?" he asked acidly. "Having been here yesterday, they might well be somewhere else today. We could be lucky. That bread smells good, Myra. And that stew! How is it coming along?"

"Ready when the lads have finished making themselves into film stars."

Dinner was almost gay, and Bony was glad, and hoped the mood would continue for forty-eight hours, although he knew it would not. Afterwards, Maddoch helped the girl to clear away the utensils, and Riddell carried the empty meat tins and refuse to the dump off the main cavern.

"There are two things I forgot," Bony said. "A tomahawk and a tin-opener. If we lose the tin-opener, we still have the tomahawk."

They thought it a great joke, and presently he felt he must hard pedal.

"You know the extent of these caverns," he said to calm them. "There are other systems adjoining these, making a very large area. Here and there on the Plain are other such areas which are avoided by stock, and at night are dangerous. You can imagine how easy it would be, in the dark, to step into that opening above us. There are countless crevices and small holes as well, waiting to break a leg, to break a neck.

"We have to walk ten miles before day-break, and it isn't possible to see if the ground underfoot is solid or cavernous. Therefore, we must proceed in single file. I will take the lead, with the dog as additional eyes. I want you to come last, Mark, and constantly check the five walking ahead of you. There is to be no talking once we stand up beyond the exit, because sound carries a long way at night when there's no wind. Repeat, please, Mark."

Brennan did so.

"If anyone has to speak, it must be as softly as possible. And, most important, if anything is dropped, or if the binding of a blanket shoe comes undone, we must all stop. I've shown you how to carry your blanket roll like the expert. I've shown you, Riddell, how to carry that water drum. So. . . . No talking. No sound for this first night. No striking of matches."

Daylight departed never so slowly as on this long long evening.

"There should be a moon until one o'clock," Bony remarked, and the sky was clear and beckoning. Finally it was now, that Bony said:

"We'll go. Jenks, you follow me; Doctor, bring the hammer and the peg with it.

They wormed through the hole in the kitchen wall, and when they came to the pinch, Jenks was told to widen it. It proved to be even less arduous than Bony had anticipated. He turned to Havant.

"Well, Doctor, this is where we part for a few days. Hold the fort. Move around. Light the lamps as usual. If those jailers come one night with supplies or another prisoner, you will need your wits. Stall if possible. If we're not tracked and brought back within four or five days, you may be sure of eventual rescue. *Au revoir!*"

They shook hands. Maddoch did so, then Brennan. The girl said:

"Be seeing you, Doctor—unprofessionally." She pressed Havant's hesitant hand, and Riddell mumbled something about having a drink together. Jenks grinned, nodded.

The cool, star-studded night illumined by the moon accepted them one by one, and it was like the return to Mother Earth from a distant dead planet. The Plain was filled with scents especially for them.

Bony, who had been quick to take Lucy into his arms that her tracks would not give a clue, counted them. He moved back and they formed into a line, tall Brennan at the end. By their shapes he knew they were burdened as he had so carefully equipped them.

When they set out, the moon was nearing the zenith

and the shadows were short. Lucy wanted to be put down, and he had to cuff her because her struggling body prevented him from seeing where to place his feet.

His mind was thus fully occupied. Those following had not to watch where to walk, save close behind the figure ahead. This world was outside their experience, even beyond their imagination. This world had no limits, no landmarks, no features to attract the eye, nothing save the moon high above, distant and cold.

At first all was fairyland, enchantment, but soon it palled by its immobility, for nothing seemed to move, even themselves, who lifted one foot and thrust it forward, and then the other to thrust it farther still. Presently the effort to walk seemed pointless, save only to keep up with the figure ahead, and why that should be necessary became pointless, too.

Bony carried the dog for the first two miles before putting her down and trusting to chance that the aborigines would not cut her tracks. For him the going was much easier, and the dog on the leash added confidence to his feet.

There is nothing worse than walking without mental distraction, and this the old timers knew when they invented the treadmill.

Twice they rested for fifteen minutes before the moon went down. After that, muscular effort, without result, was still worse. With the moon above, they had seen the shadowing shrubs sliding past their feet.

They did not approach the great wall: it rose before them to tower above and blot out half the stars. It ruled each man's mind.

No! To climb that cliff now . . . no, no.

Bony said, reassuringly:

"Made only of straw. We have to plough through

to the far side, and there we can dare to make a fire and brew tea, and afterwards to rest for a few hours. The dawn will come soon, and we have walked at least nine miles."

Chapter Twenty

ON THE NULLARBOR

THIS wall of straw was something like ten feet high and as many thick, and whether or no it was the same wall he had smashed through with the shovel some twenty miles to the west was not of interest to Bony. He tore and stamped his way through, the others following with little difficulty, and when beyond, he led them to the right for several hundred yards, and there lit a fire well away from it, the wall itself now blanketing the light from anyone north of it.

With the aid of firelight, he checked his companions' gear and found nothing missing. Then, for a psychological reason, he made them help him scoop and tramp a chamber inside the wall in which to sleep, giving the illusion of safe shelter.

He rationed himself to four hours' sleep, Lucy tethered to an ankle, and on waking found the sun gilding the fragile roof of the sleeping chamber and silvering its walls. It was not unlike being within a case woven by silkworms, the strands of straw like satin opalescence. The straw shimmered and gave forth music, the music of gentle surf beyond the mouth of a silver and gold cave, and Bony knew that the wind was rising—a blessing from the north, because a south wind might carry their scent for a mile and more to be registered by keen aboriginal noses.

The sun said it was nine o'clock as he built a fire on the ashes of the previous one, and filled the billy-can for tea.

Squatting on his heels, he tackled the problem of how long to permit his companions to sleep, in view of their present position relative to those wild aborigines.

They were now nine miles from the caverns and twelve from the desert lands where those wild men camped. Although improbable, it was still possible that the aborigines would visit the caverns about sun-rise, and might chance to cross the tracks evidencing the flight of the prisoners. It was a risk that had to be accepted.

Provided the aborigines left the desert lands' at sun-rise, and determined to return by sun-set to avoid camping on the Plain at night, their range would be up to twenty miles. And the fugitives were but twelve miles from the desert.

There must be no needless delay.

The water boiled, and tossing a handful of tea into the billy, he waited twenty seconds before removing the brew from the fire. Then, on walking to the wall, he noted that the wind was causing it to tremble, and that the sound of the 'surf' was now loud and near.

Rousing the sleepers, he told them to come to the fire for breakfast and bring everything with them.

As they emerged from the wall, each one stopped and stared, and Bony watched them to measure their first resistance to the Plain. Their eyes widened. Their faces registered the disbelief of what they saw, and he knew he could give them now no time to think. With the gear in their arms they walked stiffly to the fire.

"Thought you said we could camp all day in that straw stuff," Riddell complained. "Five minute sleep and you rouse us out."

"I could sleep for a year," yawned the girl. "What about a wash? I need it."

"No wash until we find water," Bony said. "I thought

we might camp here for a day, but the wind is now making the wall tremble, and if it rises much more, the wall will begin to move, and also we haven't come far enough to be safe. So eat and drink, and we'll move on."

They were sullen until Brennan asked how the wall came to be there. The explanation provided opportunity to distract them.

"Certainly looks like something's goin' to happen to it," Jenks surmised. He was standing, a pannikin of tea in one hand, and a meat-and-bread sandwich in the other. "Caw! So this is the Great Nullarbor Plain. Well, you can have it for mine. And if I was at sea I'd say it's goin' to blow like hell."

"Yes, we'll pack up and start before that wall rolls on and over us. We'll find a safer place than this to camp."

Bony rolled his own swag and that which the girl had to carry. He was obliged to assist the others, too, for they were not yet proficient.

"I'll carry your swag, Joe, as you will have the water," he told the big man. "Today I'll not have to carry the dog."

"Okay! Every little bit helps as the monkey said when he . . ."

"Hold my mirror for a second or two," Myra asked, and D.I. Bonaparte, F.R.M.I. steadied her small mirror while she did her hair and 'put on her face' with the aid of a tongue-moistened rag. "What a sight I am. Couldn't you find me some red ochre or something the blacks use?"

"You never know what we'll find, Myra. At the moment I find you looking well and attractive. As we walk, make a mental list of all the things you will buy at the shops."

"Yair," growled Riddell. "And I'll be thinking of all the beers I'll be buying."

"What do we use for money?" demanded Brennan,

and Maddoch cheerfully said he had money enough in a bank to keep them all drunk for a year.

On this note they listened to Bony's briefing.

"We start off in single file as we did last night. We'll walk for an hour by the sun, and then spell for a quarter of an hour. You follow me, Myra, and you, Mark, bring up the rear. Now you may talk as much as you like, even sing. In fact, singing would be a help. And don't look at the Plain too much. It will still be there this evening."

They moved off, Bony now with no sense of danger of them falling into a hole or over a cliff-like bank into another Bumblefoot Hole. The dog at first strained on the leash, and presently Bony freed her and she trotted on ahead, happy at last.

They were like a small caterpillar crawling across an aerodrome, and soon the wind found them and tore at the girl's hair, scampered through the men's hair, and when now and then Bony looked back at them they were staring across the world to the not-so-distant edge, the verge of cliff that couldn't possibly have any foundation.

Then Maddoch shouted:

"Look at the straw!"

The party stopped, to gaze in wonderment at what was happening. They could see neither the eastern nor the western limit of what appeared as a pale-yellow snake, alive and menacing, its body rippling in effort to digest a meal. Here and there it bulged towards them, at places it rolled over and over, and at no place was torn asunder. Bony knew it could roll over a man and do no hurt, but it appeared to be as weighty as molten metal. Brennan said, as though being the last man he would be the first to be trampled:

"Get on. Why wait around here?"

The wall proved to be an opportune spur, the wind coming from the rear being another, and Bony estimated their speed at almost three miles in that first hour. Then the wall appeared to be moving after them as fast as they walked, so that it was no farther back although it was smaller as the twisting action shredded it gradually, leaving a carpet of mush on the ground after it. As there was no suggestion of a spell, Bony kept moving for another hour, when two and a half miles had been added to the day's total.

A nasty day. The abos would be reluctant to move out of their camp. Good!

Continuing the next stage, they found it necessary to lean a fraction backward to counter the pressure of the wind, and walking seemed comparatively effortless. The wall followed them, not quite at their speed, until it broke, and the ends raced forward to curve inward until other portions broke and soon short sections were racing across the Plain like squadrons of golden cavalry, some moving faster than others, and often the slowest energised to run the fastest. One mass sped past the travellers, scattering its mush after it, growing swiftly smaller until it was in turn broken into bunches which formed into great balls. And the balls of straw became rapidly smaller until, with final collapse, they flattened amid the eternal saltbush.

Thus was the disintegration of one of these mighty walls of straw, and after that there was nothing to distract the travellers' attention from muscles beginning to complain now that the imagined danger was no more.

Bony espied a belt of blue-bush some hundred yards long, a small forest of trees three feet high on the sea of saltbush, and here was found shelter from the wind, but also increased heat from the sun, and small flies to torment them. Gratefully they sat on the ground, and only Maddoch assisted Bony to find dead bush with which to boil water for tea.

Jenks cursed the flies, and Riddell declared he would

go no farther this day, no matter what the flies did. Bony smiled at Maddoch, and Maddoch tried to return the smile but failed.

"Make a cigarette for Myra," Bony asked him, and squatted beside the fire and rolled one for himself.

They must have come eight miles. Eight added to nine totalled seventeen. Those swathes of straw mush would obliterate what tracks they could not avoid making, also the broken bush his companions had left without thought that eagle eyes might see and read the tale. They were still not far enough from jail to be safe from the warders.

The discomforts of this noon camp would, he hoped, be allies, and when the meal had been eaten, he relaxed, and waited for the allies to do the prodding, permitting the fire to die when the smoke of it would have kept the flies at bay. He lay with his eyes closed, and pictured the Plain dwarfed to map reading size, and placed imaginary pins to mark Patsy Lonergan's camps, and that far eastward position of the caverns. He had set out with the intention of following the third leg of a triangle, and he was confident that he was doing just this, the objective being Bumblefoot Hole, where there was water and a little food, and certain shelter.

To locate Bumblefoot Hole would be to find the needle in the stack, but there was that 'rock', that point of high land beyond the horizon which would presently give him a bearing, provided he could bring its shape to coincide with the mental picture he had retained.

The Plain was presenting a new face to this first of the summer windstorms. Coming down from the vast desert lands, it bore a light-brown dust which foreshortened still farther the encircling horizon, which painted the sun light red, which tinted with soft purple the salt-bush, and the blue-bush it shadowed royal blue. The sky was white, like the belly of a shark. And the wind was silent, save where it hissed past the ears, and this sound seemed to be within the mind, and the pressure of it against the body was as a thrust by the unseeable and the unknowable.

Riddell began to shout, and Bony opened his eyes to see the big man flailing his arms and fighting the flies, the filth of a nation streaming from his mouth in the frenzy of his desperation. Brennan said something, and in an instant they were exchanging blows. Myra looked at Bony and shrugged. Maddoch came to crouch before Bony. Tears were sliding down his dusty face and forming rivulets of light red paint. Flies were glued to the corners of his mouth, and were crawling into his nose and the corners of his eyes.

"We'll have to go back," he cried. "The caverns are better than this."

"You go forward, not backward, Clifford," Bony said sternly. "There can be no going back."

"But this. . . . I had no idea, Inspector."

Inspector! It belonged surely to a previous incarnation, and he wanted to correct it, to insist that he was 'Bony' to his friends, and he remembered then that respect, even fear, must go with command.

"What are those lunatics fighting about?" he asked coldly. Maddoch turned to watch when the combatants were separated by the stocky Jenks ambling between them and turning about as though no tax had been levied on his physical strength, to walk between them again.

"We may as well go on," Bony called. "We'll take it easy, and hope for a hole or a cave to camp in for the night. What about it?"

He risked the friendly question, yet was confident of their answer. Almost eagerly they agreed, and he handed his blanket roll to Riddell, and himself carried the half-full water drum.

The morale-slaying Plain took them instantly to itself, for they were like mariners leaving safe anchorage when leaving the belt of blue-bush. No ship under them, no steel walls about them. Soon there was no place to leave astern and no place to steam ahead.

There was only the nightmarish uniformity of flat plain kept steady by a cloudless sky. You can ride a camel, a horse, a jeep, and close your mind to this Nullarbor, find exquisite relief in the cinema programme the mind will screen. But on your feet, you have to walk with eyes open and the mind naked to reality.

And when the sun said: "I've had enough of looking at you," and turned to more interesting insects below, they had no cave, no hole in the ground, no blue-bush amid which to crouch. The sky caught fire from the sun's hot trail and the high-flung dust wove mighty draperies of scarlet before Space, shutting it out, as though blown upon by Evil itself. The colour in the folds deepened to magenta, then to black, and finally blessed night came.

One tiny spark glowed in the darkness, tended by a man who pushed together the ends of burning sticks. About him lay the blanket-cocooned figures of restless sleepers. He was contented, not by food but by the miles he had brought those restless sleepers, this day which was thankfully ended.

Chapter Twenty-One

THE LUCKY MAN

THE sun rose with a bound and looked at them suspiciously. From somewhere centre of the Nullarbor to its western edge lay six narrow shadows, and a seventh which petered out at about a mile. The seventh shadow was cast by Lucy.

There was no wind. No clouds. The air was cool, and there were no flies. It was one of those days when you wonder what the heck you are doing just where day found you. You wake, you stand up, and there you are. You wonder where you came from and where you are going. But the point is that if you are going anywhere at all, it will be by way of your sore feet which are somewhere at the end of your aching legs.

Bony inspected not detectives, but a bedraggled and dejected squad. He had to refasten Maddoch's blanket roll, and retie Myra's blanket shoe, and sling the half-empty water drum to sit comfortably into the small of his back. The squad wanted to remain there for several hours. Maddoch urged the return to the caverns.

"We are heading for a large depression named Bumble-foot Hole," was Bony's bait, "where there is water, plenty of it, and stores I left on my way north. We can camp there for a week if necessary. Now we have to keep moving because our only water supply is diminishing. So, come on!"

The girl followed after him, and Brennan again was the rear link. Presently, Brennan began: "Left, right, left, right, left . . . left . . . left." That helped quite a lot, and when Myra broke into 'Tipperary' and all joined in, it was better still. At the end of the first hour, their spirits had risen, to sink again when they realised that the rest-halt was exactly the same as the breakfast camp, only there were no empty tins or fire ash. And at the next halt they merely halted. Company awaited them at the third hour's halt—a colony of jerboa rats.

Here they made a fire and brewed a half-billy of tea, and Bony did his best to interest them in the habits of this rodent bearing the scientific name of Leporillus. Their houses were different in size and shape, but all were expertly constructed of woven bush, and all but two had roofs weighted with stones to defy the wind.

Jenks banged the side of his foot against a house, and Brennan removed the stones from the roof of another, when out sped a rodent of the size of a common rat, leaping in hops, its long hind legs and short fore-legs giving it the appearance of the genuine marsupial.

Bony allowed two hours' rest. Maddoch and Myra lay face down, pressing their eyes into their arms to defeat the flies, which were not really vicious. Only Lucy was happy. She snuffled at the rats' houses, and Brennan laughed uproariously when a rat bolted from the back door of one and a rabbit fled through the front door, and Lucy couldn't make up her mind which to chase.

Jenks was the most restless. He stood often to gaze at the Plain, eyes small, lips betraying nervous reaction to something his mind could not accept.

"How far we come today?" asked Riddell. "Only seven blasted miles! And half the day gone! We only doin' fourteen miles a day?"

"We should cover more when we become hardened, Joe." Bony said.

"Howja know we done seven miles?" pressed the big man.

"By the sun we have walked for three separate hours. Walking speed of the normal man unencumbered is two and a half miles to the hour. As we are all encumbered and weary, I am being generous in estimating our speed at only a fraction under the two and a half."

"Then how far are we from them caverns?"

"About forty miles."

"And how far to this Bumblefoot Hole you been tellin' us about?"

"I cannot say with any degree of accuracy, Joe. I am hoping it will be a little less than fifty miles."

"So!" Riddell pondered. "Oughta do it on our heads."

"Of course we'll do it. And another hundred miles beyond Bumblefoot Hole. Were you doubtful?"

"Well . . ."

"We'll get there," he was assured, and noting the glint in the blue eyes, he turned to gaze with Jenks at the absence of scenery.

"Think we bluffed the abos?" asked Brennan, sitting with Bony.

"I'll be more confident of that, say, tomorrow night. It's quite possible, you know, that they may never discover our departure. Having visited us the other day, they could think we were safe enough, and go off on their own affairs for several weeks. Think you could also carry Myra's swag this afternoon?"

"Sure!" drawled Brennan. "Anything to help a lady. Let's get going."

Left . . . right . . . left. Nothing to look at. The endless shuffle of left foot . . . right foot . . . left foot. Eyes front and directed to the heels of the man ahead. Sing! To hell with singing. Talk! What's the use? Daydream of city lights, of wallowing in beer, of a feast of women! Lights and beer and women! What in hell are they? Saltbush and jerboa rats! Crawling like lice on a two-bob bit! Better to have stayed with old doc in those caverns where there's water and no flies, no need to think, only listen to old doc's stories. Ruddy fool to take on this.

It was after four o'clock when Bony saw a shadow where none should be, a black line some five hundred yards to the right. He veered towards it, and hope was born, grew to maturity when the shadow thickened, and he saw what was a miniature Bumblefoot Hole.

Lucy ran on and disappeared, and presently they stood at the lip of a shelving bank, ending in a rocky floor sloping to the foot of a cliff at the far side. There were the shadows —of small eaves. There were a dozen old-man saltbush offering real wood instead of light brush, a fire to bake bread. If only water!

"Looks good to me," cried Mark Brennan. "A hole's better than all of this Plain."

Bony agreed, and turned to share their relief. His brows straightened in a swift frown. His eyes narrowed as their glance swept over the Plain. Sharply he asked:

"Where's Maddoch?"

They looked at each other, then down at the saltbush into the small depression less than half an acre in extent.

"When I looked back about half an hour ago, Maddoch was walking ahead of you, Jenks. What happened to Maddoch?"

The sailor's eyes opened wide, despite the flies. He regarded Bony as though being asked the most ridiculous question. He glanced at Myra Thomas: he gazed all about him, his jaw slack.

"Cliff!" he exclaimed. "He was in front of me at that.

Where's he got to? I don't know. Must be down there.
Must have got ahead of us without seeing him."

"You hit him with a rock or something?" mildly enquired
Brennan, and the subtlety of the suggestion didn't even
register.

Bony focused the picture he had seen when last he had
looked back. They had not been strictly in line of file, but
Maddoch was certainly of the number of those who followed
his lead. Everyone was walking with face down and
shoulders humped under the load carried. It was probable,
almost certain, that Jenks and Brennan who came after him
had at the same time been mentally occupied elsewhere than
on the Nullarbor Plain, and could, therefore, easily have
failed to notice Maddoch drop out.

"He's gone back to the caverns," guessed the girl. "Said
he wanted to. The idiot."

"Ought to see him," shouted Jenks, staring to the east,
and Brennan agreed, although he gazed to the west, and
Riddell, catching the idea, looked to the north.

Bony was sure he could see any object within three miles,
as high as Maddoch stood. Half an hour back, when he had
seen Maddoch with the party, they were about a mile, or a
little more, from this place where he was missed.

Assuming that Maddoch had dropped out without being
seen, and having the intention of returning to the caverns,
he would start walking to the north, simply because it was
opposite to the line of march. But not for long would he
continue northwards. Within minutes he would veer to the
left or the right, according to which leg was longer than the
other.

There being no natural objects to guide him, to lure him,
he would inevitably walk in a circle, the problem being how
far would Maddoch walk before making a halt, after which
he would set off on another circle.

That he, Bony, could see a walking man clearly for three miles meant little on this tricky Plain, where distance is distorted, and sound judgment not possible.

"You must camp and I'll go back to look for him." Bony led the way down to the floor of the hole. They helped to make a fire, and then Bony, noticing that Lucy's muzzle was wet, found a rock-hole half-filled with water, and covered with green slime.

"You may use this water sparingly to wash with" he said, "but not to drink unless first boiled. Brennan, I am placing the drum of clean water in your charge. You see that bush?"

"Yes."

"If I am not back by sun-rise tomorrow, make a fire under it. Make a smoke. Understand?"

"Yes, but . . . you can't leave us like this. What'll we do if you can't find your way back?"

"Yes, what'll we do, Inspector?" echoed Jenks. "If Maddoch chooses to clear out, let him go. He's askin' for what he gets."

"Too right! Too ruddy right!" snarled Riddell. "Let him rot."

Bony stared at each man, stared them down.

"Leave Maddoch. I can't leave Maddoch. I don't yet know who murdered Mitski, and I'm taking Mitski's murderer all the way."

It is said that a man spends his life struggling to return to the protection of the womb, and it was this impulse which drove the little man who loved peace and security to seek the mother he had lost when as a small child he was left, sensitive and alone. He married, not the comforter, the protective mother, but a shrew, and the climax of the tragedy was inevitable.

For Maddoch first the legal jail and then detention in the caverns had provided protection from the raw world he had feared. Although he would never admit it, even to himself, the period spent in jail had been the happiest of his life, and that spent in the Nullarbor caverns had given much in compensation for the unnecessary crudities. The craving for protection afforded by the known caverns had reached its peak when gazing upon the tiny houses of the jerboa rats.

Inspector Bonaparte wouldn't turn back, so he decided he must slip away and seek the warm comfort and safety of those caverns where there were no flies, no glaring sun, no torturing left, right, left, right.

Gradually he edged himself out of the line; slowly he fell back, the last two men passing without lifting their heads. For a moment he stood watching them. Then he realised that at any moment the leader might see him standing there like a fool. Down he went to sprawl amid the salt-bush, to lie still.

Then he was running. The run became a trot, the trot a hurried walk. He glanced backward. The party had vanished. He was free to walk on and on to where Dr. Havant waited. Dr. Havant would be so pleased to see him, so happy to hear that Clifford Maddoch couldn't bear to think of the doctor being so alone, and had come back to keep him company.

Presently he was conscious that the sun had disappeared. H'm! Must have come a long way. Can't be much farther to go. He tripped and fell hard on his chest, scrambled up and gazed about with bovine curiosity for what had snared his foot.

However, it wasn't so important, and he had yet to find Dr. Havant. The evening brought the horizon closer, and it was so quiet that he could hear the soft swish when a foot brushed a bush. Then it was suddenly moonlight, and he knew he must be close to the caverns for he had crawled from the caverns into the moonlight.

Following this thought a sound far away came rushing upon him, engulfing him within a voice that screamed. He didn't recognise the cry of the brolga.

He was lying on the ground. He could feel the cool touch of saltbush under his face. He was running; he knew he was running; knew he was crawling on hands and knees, was certain he was drawing nearer and nearer to the little hole down which he would crawl to Dr. Havant. That little hole! Maddoch shrieked with mirth. His wife would never be able to crawl into that little hole. She was too big, too damn big, the screaming bitch.

The moon was up there, too. For a long time he gazed at her, but the moon persisted in moving so that he had to turn his head when it was painful to do so. Blast the moon! He closed his eyes and the moon was gone, and it was daylight. He was looking along his arm. He could see his hand resting on the ground, palm upward. And beyond his hand stood a kangaroo, cleaning its face with a paw, like a cat.

A kangaroo! Perhaps Dr. Havant would know how to kill it and they could eat its tail. Kangaroo soup was a luxury for sure. Once he had tasted some at a dinner somewhere. The kangaroo took no notice of him, didn't see him. That's funny! The kangaroo came and sniffed at his finger-tips. Well, now! How extraordinary! The kangaroo actually jumped up and now sat right on his hand.

It was perfect from nose to tail. The colour of its coat was fawn and there was a tiny streak of white down its soft warm belly. Maddoch, with strange violence, closed his hand and imprisoned the kangaroo.

Sitting up without opening his hand, and this was done with spasmodic effort, Maddoch gazed at the tail of the prisoner and chuckled gleefully at the prize he would present to the lonely Havant. He tried to stand, failed, and tried again, continuing to hold the kangaroo in his closed hand. A foot appeared in front of him, and he looked up to see his wife. He opened his mouth to scream, and the woman became Inspector Bonaparte, who said:

"A pair of giant compasses would not have drawn a better circle for me to follow than you did with your feet, Clifford. Come along, now. Get up, and we'll find the camp where there'll be coffee waiting, and something to eat."

An arm lifted him. He knew his burning feet were dragging.

"Where were you when Mitski was killed, Clifford?" the persuasive voice asked, and only after many attempts to speak did he say:

"Coming from the Jeweller's Shop, Inspector. I saw him near the boulder."

"You didn't kill him, did you?"

"No. How could I? I wasn't . . ."

"Of course not, Clifford. Now lift your feet and help a little. We haven't far to go. Out on the Nullarbor Plain so bright, we're so happy we could be tight. I'll help you and you'll help me, and we'll go forward with hearts of glee. Didn't know I am a poet, did you?"

"I . . . I want to find the caverns and the doctor, Inspector."

"Not now, Clifford. We're on the Nullarbor. Not in, but on Australia, the real Australia known by the aborigines, the old time sundowners, the stockmen and waifs like us. For people in cars who follow the roads, for politicians who come inland only when winter coolness is here, Australia puts on a disguise. You and I see Australia without any disguise, see Australia as it really is. You have a great deal to be joyful about.

"Come on, lift your feet. That's better. You will come to love Australia, as I do. You have to get down on your stomach, press your face into the sand and against the hot gibbers, smell the land and feel through your empty belly its closeness to you, woo it with a voice clogged by the lack of saliva. And then, Clifford, as with many men, this naked fair Australia will become the great love of your life."

How far! What was that the Inspector said. What?

"What have you in your hand, Clifford? Show me."

A blessed halt, and Maddoch opened his hand.

"See, you have already captured the veritable Australia. Don't you know that scientists, writers and photographers travel around Australia in trucks and caravans, and never ever see, let alone hold in their hands, a kangaroo mouse. You lucky, lucky man."

Chapter Twenty-Two

AGAIN THE PLAIN ATTACKS

THEY trudged in line abreast to prevent delay like that occasioned by Maddoch. At the beginning of the trek it had been essential to follow-my-leader to minimise risk of injury. Then it became necessary for the leader to set a pace to outwit possible pursuit, and, when that menace lessened, speed remained an important factor, as the food and water supplies were so limited.

Maddoch's condition compelled them to camp for one day in the shallow depression where, fortunately, Lucy had found water. After the day's rest, Maddoch was well enough to proceed, and the new order of march, although slower, was conducive to the maintenance of morale.

Bony persuaded them to sing, and when they tired of this, he induced Brennan to act the sergeant-major by calling the steps. This suited Brennan. Riddell grumbled incessantly. Jenks now and then hopped over a bush instead of ploughing through it, and his nimbleness prompted Bony to ask if he had done any tap-dancing.

"Not the real thing," replied Jenks. "Me old man usta think I'd make a fighter good enough to keep him in whisky, and he paid gym fees and lost his dough and drank himself to death 'fore I could get into real class. Still, I learned how to take care of meself against the Liverpool Irish, and they're the boys what make a man step lively. What d'you reckon, Joe?"

"You ain't so bad, Ted. T'hell with these flies."

In the afternoon of the next day, Bony was relieved of anxiety by a faint blue knob of high land, far to the west, and he was confident that his general line of progress was accurate. At sun-down, when they had to camp on the open Plain, the knob was banished by the glare, but after the sun had gone, it stood in bold relief and was identical with the mental picture retained of its shape.

The following morning, therefore, he altered course and steered due south for Bumblefoot Hole.

The wind came, but not with the fierceness of the storm that disintegrated the straw wall. It blew from the west and filled the sails of small individual clouds, and sped their shadows over the silvered floor of the Plain, emphasising the insecurity of the nebulous world.

"We should reach Bumblefoot Hole today," he told his companions. "We'll then be about halfway home. We'll be able to camp there for two days, rest and repair our footwear, bathe and wash clothes, and generally prepare for a good start on the second leg of the journey."

"That sounds glorious to me," said Myra, who was walking beside him. Although he carried her swag and he had maintained her blanket footwear, she was excessively tired, but unflaggingly spurred by the attractive carrot of fame dangling before her eyes.

"We could miss Bumblefoot Hole," Bony warned. "Although much bigger than that other hole we camped in, we could pass it by within a quarter of a mile especially on a day like this when the cloud shadows are moving so fast. So keep your eyes open, all of you."

"When ought we to come to it?" pressed Myra, and Jenks the sailor snarled:

"Cawl Give the Inspector a chance. You take a bearin' on that queer sort of rock on the skyline, Inspector?"

Bony replied that he had.

"Well, then, Myra, how in 'ell d'you think the Inspector can tell you what time he'll reach port when there ain't nothin' for him to take a cross bearin' on? Look, if we hit this Bumblefoot Hole he'll be a ruddy marvel, that's what he'll be."

Brennan tentatively suggested that they should head for the land, meaning the rock of high ground.

"Bad country, Mark," Bony explained. "Low scrub trees, sand, saltpans, desert, without water, nothing for two thousand miles, and then the Indian Ocean."

They were resting in the mid-morning when Brennan insisted they should make for the high land, and so get away from the Plain, speaking with a sharp quaver in his voice. When Maddoch firmly reiterated what Bony had said, Brennan knocked him down. Whereupon Riddell took Maddoch's part, and Jenks sprang to his feet. The girl said, irritably:

"That's right, tear each other to bits, you whiskery baboons, you unwashed heroes. Plenty of fight, but full of moans and groans at having to do a little walking. Shut up! You make me sick!"

"You'd of been sicker by this time in them caverns with old Doc Havant," yelled Jenks, whose whiskers, instead of lying respectably close to his face, stood out like the quills of an angry porcupine, and Bony was thankful that there were no baboons in Australia. He said, as though directing rebellious children:

"We'll confine our energy to lifting one foot, then the other, and repeat the movement. That's the way."

An eternity later the sun said one o'clock, and, when a cloud threatened, they camped an hour for lunch, bodies aching and nerves ragged, and as the afternoon wore on, even the prospect of Bumblefoot Hole, with all its promised amenities, failed to rouse them from a mood of sullen silence that no amount of cheerful urging by Bony could even penetrate. The shadows worried him, presenting an additional problem, for often he was obliged to stop to assure himself that a shadow was not actually Bumblefoot Hole.

Then at four o'clock when they were resting, Brennan's nerve broke. He stood up, focused the blue rock of the distant upland, and walked off towards it.

"Where the hell you going?" shouted Riddell.

"Come back here, you cranky lunatic," yelled Jenks.

Brennan turned and shouted abuse. He went on, walking towards that land of terrible certainty, of death.

"Quiet," Bony ordered. "Wait. Just watch him."

Brennan had gone a hundred yards, and as they waited and watched, he covered the second hundred yards. Two hundred yards isn't far on the Nullarbor Plain, where you believe you can see for fifty miles. Bony, on back-tracking the vanished Maddoch, found that he had been only a thousand yards from the place where he was missed, yet none had seen him.

Watching Brennan at two hundred yards, they saw the edge of a cloud shadow race upon him, seemingly engulf him, and in the comparative blackness of the shadow, he abruptly waved his arms wildly, and fell on his chest.

"Now what's wrong with him?" Jenks demanded aggrievedly.

The shadow left Brennan and pounded upon them. Dust was rising near the prostrate man. Wisps of saltbush about him appeared to be flung upwards.

"Remain here. I'll fetch him," Bony said, and when half-way to Brennan, he turned to be sure they were obeying him.

Brennan had dug little holes for his fingers to cling

to. He was lying flat, and the toes of his rag-protected feet were dug hard into the earth. His face between the reaching arms was pressed against the dust. His head was to the west, toward yet another cloud shadow racing to them.

"Brennan! Get up!" ordered Bony. "Come, Brennan! On your feet."

Brennan scrabbled harder against the Plain, and Bony thudded a fist between his shoulders.

"No . . . no!" Brennan shouted without lifting his head. "Get down . . . get down quick . . . you'll be spun off into space."

"No chance, Mark. Sit up. It's all right. It's only the clouds making the world seem to spin. Now get up! Bumblefoot Hole is only just ahead."

With a swift motion, Bony tossed Brennan over upon his back, as he might a turtle on the beach. Brennan's eyes were closed and he refused to open them. Lucy came and licked his face, and that did open his eyes. He was panting, less from fatigue than terror, and Bony assisted him to his feet, supporting him while his eyes slowly lost their glaze. Presently he could stand without support, and for a little while passed a hand to and fro across his eyes, and looked at Bony with puzzled dismay.

"God! That was the chips, Inspector. I couldn't hold on. The earth was going overboard faster and faster. I can't tell you. . . . You don't know . . ."

"Actually I do," he was assured. "I've felt it too. You are imaginative, like me, and the Plain can make fools of us in countless ways. The imaginative man will more quickly become lost than the unimaginative, but it is men blessed with imagination who climb Everests and cross Nullarbors. Feeling better?"

Brennan nodded. He gazed about as though determined to test himself. Again looking at the slight figure with him, and meeting the blue eyes, he said:

"You're a good bloke, pal. I'm all right now. If I act wonky again, clout me one."

"I'll heave the water drum at you if I happen to be carrying it, Mark. I knew a fellow once who used to say when things were bad, 'Nothing for it but hard smoking.' We can say, 'There's nothing for it but hard walking.' By the way, just where were you when Mitski was killed?"

"Me! In the passage to the blow-hole. I told you that."

"Myra was with you, wasn't she?"

"Yes. She lost her scarf up the blow-hole that time."

"What were you two doing there?"

"Me?" again Brennan asked inanely. "I was trying to soften her up. What a hope."

"Why did you go there?"

"Matter of fact, she'd been leading Mitski on a bit, and things weren't too good. Doc dressed Jenks down for something he said. I didn't hear what it was. That was the night before. I told Myra I wanted to talk serious. She went with me, and after I told her where she was likely to get off if she went on making out she liked one better than the rest, she sort of made me think she only liked me. Then when I acted on that, she went crook. That was when we heard Mitski yelling."

"It was as well I was tossed down among you, Mark."

"Yair. I'll tell you something, Inspector, although it's not up my alley, and the blokes in Goulburn would call me for everything. The rock Mitski was killed with, Myra found on her bed the same morning. Told me she found it, anyway. I chucked it down Fiddler's Leap."

He had chucked it down Fiddler's Leap—the blunt instrument of murder. Just like that. Why? Because the blokes in Goulburn would call him for everything if he aided a police officer. Now for the confidence, when association in hardship and unity of objective was breaking down one loyalty and building another.

"Was there blood on the rock?" Bony asked.

"Yair. A smear in one place. It killed Mitski all right."

"When did Myra discover the rock on her bed?"

"When, Inspector?" Brennan frowned under compulsion to exercise his mind. "She did say, 'cos I asked her. I know. It was after she'd done the breakfast things."

"She didn't mention it to me, Mark."

"I told her not to."

"Why?"

"Oh, you know how it is. Blimey! You must know."

"Perhaps I do. Whoever murdered Mitski tried to place the blame on Myra. Unless Myra committed the murder and told you a tale about finding the rock on her bed."

"Could be either way, Inspector. Why worry at it? Mitski's dead. Body's well down under. Let it lie, let it lie."

They joined the party and Bony explained that Brennan had been attacked by giddiness. No one said anything, but the expression he caught in the eyes of the girl and Maddoch told him they understood what he meant, and warned him they would need watching.

Forward. Effort without motive. You walk a street and there is a lamp standard ahead to walk to, to pass, to leave behind you. Something is always happening. Nothing happened here save the speeding cloud shadows, and for them you ought to be grateful. You came from nowhere, and you are going to nowhere, for nowhere isn't a place or a thing. You count your steps: a hundred, a thousand, a million, and you are on the same spot you were on in the beginning.

The sun took the road to the highland serrating the western horizon. The clouds dried up, first the little clouds.

Human shadows lengthened. Clouds! So what! Shadows! So what! Go on, feet! Go on. . . . Step over this bloody bush, feet!

Abruptly Bony stopped. Automatically they halted, to find him looking at Lucy. The dog's nose was pointing south of west. Her thin tail trembled. She glanced back, and Bony called:

"Go on . . . sool 'em!"

Lucy veered to follow the line of her nose—the scent her nose was registering. They followed, and now and then she signalled with her tail.

The cloud shadows had gone, but another appeared ahead, a shadow which thickened, lengthened.

"What's she sniffin' at?" asked Riddell, and Brennan replied:

"Roast beef and Yorkshire pudding and parsnips and brussels sprouts."

"Could be at that," sniggered Jenks.

The commander felt obliged to retain respect. He said:

"I have been wondering who would first see Bumblefoot Hole. I thought I would have to point it out, but Lucy saved me the trouble. It's just ahead. And friends of mine are waiting to welcome us. Like Lucy, I can scent them."

Chapter Twenty-Three

HALF-WAY INN

THEY stood silent, four men and a woman numbed by fatigue, and Bony justly proud of having brought them thus far. They watched Lucy leaping like a goat down to the floor of Bumblefoot Hole, and run like a hare to meet the camels, who greeted her with lofty, albeit warm, affection.

"Well, there it is," Bony said, cheerfully. "We'll have to go round the rim to take the only path down. This place may not appear to you as such, but to me it looks and feels like home."

Millie regarded them with assumed unconcern, but Curley spread his rear legs and closed his fore-legs in the un-mistakable gesture of impatience. On arriving at the old fireplace, they flung their packs and the water drum from weary bodies, and slumped to the ground.

It was Bony who made the fire and set a billy of water against it.

These four men who had withstood jail routine, and as successfully resisted the utter boredom of confinement in Nature's dungeons, were now rapidly deteriorating. The woman was still driven by iron determination to survive that she might enjoy rewards she had certainly not earned, and she had been least affected by the Plain. True, Bony had saved her as much as possible, which she had taken for granted, causing him to ponder on the ruthless urge to batten on everyone for her own advantage.

She was sitting now with her eyes closed, still fighting the effects of the odds against her from both the Plain and Bony's leadership. Jenks merely stared about. Mark Brennan sighed with relief from an ordeal having nothing to do with weariness, and Maddoch had sprawled forward to bury his face in his arms.

Under the circumstances, they had done remarkably well these last few days, when the ground covered had been nearer twenty than fifteen miles per day.

Bony was pouring tea when Lucy came to tell him that both she and the camels were thirsty. He gave her water in the crown of his old felt hat, but foresaw that watering the camels would be difficult. On explaining the difficulty to Riddell, that gentleman said the camels could rot, and this released a violent tirade from Myra, explosively betraying the state of her nerves.

Lucy having failed to aid them, Millie led Curley forward to make known their protest. Now without fettering hobbles, she stalked silently to the camp and stuck her muzzle into the empty billycan. The interested Curley romped through the group, scattering them wildly, and nuzzled the packs as though he could smell bread crusts. And then he stretched his long neck in appeal to Bony, his twitching split upper lip so dry and hot and needing water, his large black eyes pleading.

Bony again called for assistance, and surlily they gave it. It meant keeping the animals at bay with sticks while Bony dipped, with a half-gallon can, about eight gallons of water from the rock-hole to a rock-basin.

The sun had gone to bed and dusk was shrouding Bumblefoot Hole when they had eaten. Bony suggested a cave apiece and sleep, and neither Riddell nor Jenks needed further prompting. Maddoch was almost uncon-scious, and Brennan dragged him off to another cave, where he rolled him into his blanket and settled into his own.

Then all was quiet and darkening. The camels were down and Bony was weighing in his hands the bag containing the remainder of the flour.

"Off to bed for you too," he told Myra firmly. "There's a cave over there just right for you."

"What are you going to do?"

"Bake bread when the fire burns down. How are your feet?"

"Still sore. They need a wash. I need a wash all over. Could I put water into the rock-basin and really wallow?"

"Yes, water's plentiful. I'll bale some out of the hole for you."

"Would I be safe, d'you think?"

"Of course. The camels won't hurt you."

"I wasn't thinking of the camels, Inspector."

"Well, the men are all tucked up."

"All except one," she said, faintly pert.

Anger slowly welled to flush his dark forehead, and his eyes blazed. Saying nothing, he took the can to the waterhole and baled. The girl crouched beside the fire until he came and snatched up a blanket, taking it to the hole and fashioning a rough screen.

She was away for half an hour. She was refreshed of body, and Bony hoped also of mind. He said:

"Stay awhile. I want to talk to you. You need not waste your time on sex innuendo. It's a language I do not understand." He stirred the loaf baking in the ashes and decided it required further time. "When Mitski was killed, where were you?"

"I told you, Inspector. In the kitchen."

She was perfectly composed.

"I recall that is what you told me, but where were you?"

"Well, I can only . . ."

"I want the truth, Myra. Why are you opposed to admitting that you were with Mark Brennan in the passage to the blow-hole?"

"Because I don't want to admit I was alone with any one of those murderers, that's why. I suppose Brennan crowed about it."

"No. I knew you must have been there, because the draught trapped your scarf and it led me to the outlet above.

"When we reach a civilised point, we shall be surrounded by police and Security men—the latter because it is thought your disappearance was deliberate, and for the purpose of spying into secrets of the rocket range. I can clear you with a word, or I can, and will, have you held for weeks on suspicion—of murder."

She was stilled, and the flickering firelight danced in her fathomless eyes.

"I want the murderer of Igor Mitski," he went on. "It's up to you to clear yourself. From whom, or from what, did you evolve the theory that Mitski's murderer planned to kill all rivals, so as to be the only lion in the den?"

"It was Havant's idea. He predicted it would happen, and when we were all looking at Mitski and knew he'd been murdered, he said, 'Who's next?'"

"Did you kill Mitski?"

"Of course not. He was quite harmless, like you."

"Do you know who did?"

"Why? Should I?"

"Answer me. Including Mitski, there were six men with you. Who, assuming he was the only one left with you, would you fear most of those six?"

"Riddell."

"Who, under those circumstances, would you choose to be left with, again assuming you intended to preserve your chastity?"

"So modestly put," she mocked. "I could name Maddoch, but . . . some spiders bite and some don't."

"Then you think it possible that Maddoch killed Mitski?"

"Yes. Riddell accused Maddoch, but then Riddell's just an animal. I'll tell you this, dear Inspector. Any one of them would have attacked me if they hadn't been afraid of being killed in the rush. I like it that way."

"You include Doctor Havant?"

"I wouldn't agree to stay behind with him, would I?"

Bony raked the loaf from the ashes, and rebuilt the fire for another loaf. She watched him warily.

"What d'you hope to do when you're free of the Plain . . . and of me?" he asked.

"The Press boys will be around, and plenty. I've got it all plotted, provided you don't spoil the show. The men will say their little pieces, never fear. But I'll work on the angle of the hen among the roosters. They can't say they seduced me. I'll tell how I out-witted their persistent efforts. That *will* be news. I could mention how I had to resist you, but I won't, because there's a lot about you that my grandmother would admire. I know a man in Melbourne who's the king of publicity agents. I'll script the lot for U.S.A Radio, and go over there to appear on T.V., and he won't hesitate to back a brave girl. Australia can go hopping. It can buy my leavings from America, same as it buys the leavings of all American and English top-liners. The art is to withhold to create demand. I have the art, plus."

Bony could easily believe her about mastery of the art of withholding. He spoke ironically:

"It seems we shall not be treading on each other's toes."

"Is that all you have to say? Good-night, Inspector. I hope you trust me now."

"On all counts excepting the killing of Mitski."

"Ye Gods! You remind me of Nemesis."

"Others before you have been so reminded. Good-night, Myra."

He continued to squat on his heels, damping the fire to conserve the precious supply of wood, and he watched the little holes appear in the fine ash atop the baking loaf, and the tiny spurts of steam erupting from them. The fine ash covering the graveyard of his mind broke open, and a voice from the past said: "She's a tough item."

Myra Thomas was a tough item. Her trial for murder hadn't softened her. Her trials in the caverns hadn't reduced the toughness. It must have been there at birth, and no Pygmalion could have done anything about it.

Well, he would give these people a day's spell, for the Plain would tax them and wear them down even more. He foresaw explosive situations which would tax all his acumen, and the condition of these people when those situations arose would be that of utter exhaustion. It was, of course, impossible to place any trust in Myra Thomas. She would continue to use them all when it suited her, and so additional physical hardship for her wouldn't be amiss.

Lucy came to him and stood gazing hopefully. She had fed well, and could have wanted for nothing. Shortly afterwards, movement behind him made him swivel about, and there stood the two camels, heads low, the upper lip of each lifting like the nostrils of hungry men smelling a delicious dinner. They had been good companions. They might still be. He pondered on whether they could carry the girl and Maddoch without the riding saddles, and concluded it might be managed but would be fraught with difficulties which would cause dangerous delay, so decided against it.

On digging the loaf from the ashes, he set it end up against the billy-can to steam dry, and broke off pieces from the first loaf for the dog to carry to the waiting Millie and Curley.

Having placed the bread where the camels could not get at it, he baled water for himself and bathed. Later, he took his blanket to the shelter of a distant boulder, and there tied the dog to an ankle, and slept the clock round. The sun was friendly when he woke to see the others about the camp fire, and to find the camels missing.

He was greeted almost cheerfully. Later in the morning when they were still disposed to loll about, he advised them to bathe and wash their clothes, as they would have to move on next morning.

Brennan and Riddell objected.

"It would be wise for all of you to stay here until I can obtain transport," he urged, and was instantly opposed. "Well, it's up to you, individually. Before sun-rise to-morrow I shall be leaving."

Riddell continued to grumble, but Brennan surrendered with good heart, as did Jenks. Maddoch was silent, and would still need supervision.

During the afternoon he offered his worn riding boots to Myra, who found she could wear them when her feet were protected with strips of blanket. He did what he could to mend the footwear of the others, who now knew what the saltbush could do to naked feet.

When the sun rose the next morning, Bumblefoot Hole was a full mile behind them.

Chapter Twenty-Four

THE PLAIN'S LAST ASSAULT

ONE? Two? How many days ago was it when we rested for hours and hours at that dump the Inspector had called Bumblefoot Hole? What the Hell! He wouldn't look at the ruddy Plain. That was no use. Nothing to see, nothing but that precipice at the end, and the feeling of being pushed over it. There wasn't even any clouds to look at, and looking at Joe and Ted and moody old Clifford was like looking at himself.

Mark Brennan tramped. He was tired of whispering to himself 'left, right, left'. But he could still hear it and it wasn't his voice shouting. He recalled the voice, the man and the place. The place was a road bordered by green paddocks. There were roadside gums, and in the distance were green hills. The man was a sergeant marching beside a squad of fellers like himself. He had ribbons, too, the sarge had, medals from War One.

A good mob that was. Lot of 'em got killed, and some perished as prisoners of war. Pity he hadn't gone off with 'em. Pity he'd lost his block over that wench. The bitch! Him doing his duty by the country, and her rushing to marry that schemer who had no intention of fighting, going to stay on the farm and make lots of dough out of black markets and things.

He had stopped 'em all right. They thought themselves lookin' good when they came out of that church. Still, addin' it all up, it was a bloody silly thing to do. Not worth being kept in the jug when the mob was overseas bein' kind to the girls and fightin' the enemy in their spare time. Not worth a lot of other things too. He could have let 'em alone, and in time that bitch would have given the husband hell without any assistance from Private Mark Brennan.

Not worth breakin' up the old man like it did, either. Decent old bloke, too. The old lady had taken it bad, but she'd stuck it out, and carried on the farm and was waiting for him to go back and help her out. Would have done it, too, if he hadn't been shanghai'd into those caverns. Still, better late than never. Now he was on his way to the farm and the old lady, perhaps. On his way? What way? Go on, keep your feet up. Pick 'em up, there! Pick 'em up! All right, Sarge! All right!

Good bloke that sergeant, what's his name? Decent warders, too. Some of 'em crook, but not many. Most of 'em would give a bloke a fair go. The Governor, too. Wished him luck. Would have got home if he hadn't fell for that skirt drivin' the car, and took her on when she offered him a lift. If he met her again, he'd choke her. Offerin' him a nip of coffee royal and doping him well and truly. Choke her to death! Hey, wait, Mister Mark Brennan. None of that. You've had all that. You got to lay flowers on the old man's grave and look after the old woman from here on.

Left, right! Ease up, Sarge! I'm goin' through. Don't worry. Goin' through this damn bloody Plain with Inspector Bonaparte. Inspector Bonaparte! He's all right. Once on a feller's tracks, just like the Tasmanian tiger cat, never leaves 'em. Good feller, too. Bloody good feller. Would have been sunk if it wasn't for him. Tire him out! What a hope! Did you ever see eyes like that, Mark, you rotten swine? Did you? "What's that, Clifford? What did you say?"

"Nothing, Mark. Nothing at all." What is there to say? I have to be careful with my feet. I have to think where to put them, and that makes lifting them up even more of an effort. Don't interrupt, Mark, please. Not now. If you do you might make me forget to lift up my feet and put them down, and then I'll never walk again. How could I? What book was that in? Never mind the title. The writer said that everyone was destined to walk this earth, and was given a number of the steps he would take before he laid himself down with exquisite relief and died. Do you know what? I think that very soon I shall reach the allotted number of my steps, years before my time.

Zombie! Freda called me a zombie. I certainly felt like one when she kept on and on screaming into my mind. I wouldn't have been so desperate if only she hadn't screamed. And to say all those things in my own office, with Kendal and Mace listening. To repeat them over and over that night we left the Urban Committee Meeting. What the men thought I could see in their faces.

I tried to be merciful. I wouldn't have given her strychnine had I known its terrible effects. I could have given her cyanide instead. Now, Clifford Maddoch! Don't forget to raise your feet and put them down—this one, that one, this one, that one. That's it, Clifford. Inspector Bonaparte is doing this. He doesn't forget. He doesn't forget anything.

How stupid I was to crush that little kangaroo mouse. I could have kept it in a pocket, then sent it to a taxidermist in Sydney and had it stuffed, and no one could ever say I hadn't been in the real Australia, could they? Pity Mitski died. Funny that his voice was so like my wife's. Mitski would have composed a tune to that little kangaroo mouse. Now he's down somewhere in Fiddler's Leap. Fiddler's

Leap! Bumblefoot Hole! Big Claypan! Curley's Hate!
What curious names.

I'll make twelve more steps before I look up to see if
there's anything to see. One, two, three . . . ten, eleven,
twelve. Nothing. Nothing at all except the saltbush, and
the sky. Two things. I'll try that again. I'll make it twenty-
four before I look up. "Sorry, Riddell. I wasn't laughing at
you."

Ruddy squirt. Always hated the cocky jumped-up.
Bashed old Mitski, he did. Saw him doing it. Like a cock
sparrer the way he's moving. If he'd been a man like me,
Joe Riddell, he wouldn't have fed poison to his missus; he'd
have picked her up by the feet and cracked the backyard
cement with her head. Could always say she fell outer the
upstairs winder. Oughta had more brains meself, come to
sum it up. Shootin' that cocky for moanin' about the cow
was a bit raw. Nothin' to be proud of. I shoulda pushed
him up into the fork of a tree and left him with his neck in
the fork. Could've explained how he went climbin' trees
lookin' for bees' nests.

Gord! How much more of this? Week after week walk-
in' to nothin', that's what we're doin'. Shoulda stayed
behind with old Havant. Woulda, too, if that slut had
stayed. I'd have found out what she was made of.

Crikey! That land over there looks different to what it
was yestiday. Must be movin' along it. There's a rabbit.
Ain't seen a rabbit after that one what done a bunk from
them sticks and things Mark stirred up. Eat! I'd eat him fur
an' all. When I get off this ruddy Plain I'll get the lend of a
hundred quid off Maddoch—have to talk cobber-like—and
I'll buy a hundred loaves of bread, half a side of beef, two
sides of bacon, ten dozen eggs, and I'll hole up somewhere.
No more farmers for me. No more livin' with cows.
Wimmen! To hell with wimmen. Grub . . . tucker . . .

food . . . that'll be all I'll ever want. I'll eat, and eat, and eat.

The sun rises in the east, sets in the west . . . ran the mind of Edward Jenks. Can't bluff me. Makin' south, all right. Getting closer to that land all the time. The d. knows his onions, give him his due. More sting in him than all the rest in the bag. Caw! Joe's all in, the big slob. Mark's wobblin' like a drunk, and Clifford couldn't run a yard if his missus turned up.

That leaves me. Tough Ed, they called me. Well, I ain't done so bad at that. Lotta life in the old dog, as I'll show 'em—an' that trollop, when I get me chance. No woman puts it over me like Cliff's missus did. Come to think it all out, that leaves this ruddy cop what calls himself a Detective-Inspector. Got a reputation they say. So has Mister Edward Jenks, Esquire, A.B. Different method, that's what. Another day, maybe two, an' we arrives some place. Then we all start again on scratch, and if ever I happen to meet that Myra Thomas on a dark street, well, well, what do we say, Mister Jenks and Missus Thomas?

The nights now were mere interludes. The rest periods ordered by Bony were without reality. Myra Thomas existed on her dreams of power and glory. Jenks looked up now and then, not at the Plain which was battering them into themselves, but at the lurching figure of the female shape in male attire. None of them even noticed the crows that came to meet them from the 'coast', as though they were doves leading them to the land and trees where they roosted o' nights, safe from wild dogs and foxes.

The following day was to be the last day of this trek, and during the afternoon they skirted the coast, travelling from one promontory to the next. Bony watched the sun, maintained a check of time, and camped that night in the shelter of a small 'island' on which grew a few mulgas. They had one tin of meat and two of fish, and that was the end of the food supply.

Argument arose because three tins could not serve as plates for six people.

"Caw! What am I goin' to eat out of?" snarled Jenks, and the girl said, contemptuously:

"Be your natural self. Eat off the ground, of course."

Jenks glanced at Riddell as though expecting support. Bony quickly suggested a pannikin in lieu of a golden platter, and emptied half a tin of herrings in tomato sauce into a pannikin for himself, and presented the other half in its tin to Myra, saying:

"At our last camp we still had plates and forks, you will remember. Someone has left them behind. Now we have only our fingers."

"Which will serve Ted for the rest of his life," sneered the girl.

"Ain't we gettin' snooty, Myra? Next week we'll be seein' Mrs. Myra Thomas, the famous ex-murderess, a-strollin' down Pitt Street. And no one will be thinkin' that the lovely on the prance lived with a lot of men on a Plain where there's never no bush nor a tree to hide it. Will you be tellin' your dear public about *all* the terrors you went through?"

"I'll tell my public all about you, Jenks. About how you eat like the guzzling pig that you are."

"And how you was the hen with all the roosters, I suppose. How you fought off the roosters and saved it? And how you bumped off your husband because he found out you're sexless, like Doc Havant said. I could've fixed that. Woman! Caw! You ain't a woman. You're all blah and bilk. Why, them ten-bob-a-timers in the back alleys off the water-front is more a woman than you. You wasn't even born a female. Wait till I have my little say on the wireless."

"You won't. They're particular about keeping the air clear of microbes."

"What about calling it a day?" complained Maddoch. "No one enjoys listening to your polite conversation."

"Don't you butt in, Clifford. You know how this cow played us all against each other. You know how she worked us up so that someone bashed poor old Mitski. She could've done him in only she was being raped by Mark at the time, wasn't she, Mark?"

"Don't drag me into it," pleaded Brennan. "I'm too leg-weary even to think about it. Give us peace . . . peace . . . and more peace. Why the hell were women invented?"

"Lovely liars," drooled Jenks. "Smooth legs 'n soft beds. I just itch to see 'em again, not havin' seen a woman for years. I . . ."

"It will be even more years before any of you again see women, lovely or otherwise, if you forget to obey me when we reach this homestead," Bony interrupted. "There are white men and white women, and we shall be dependent on them for food, clothes and transport to the railway. You may even recognise someone who was instrumental in your kidnapping, and should you lose your temper and do anyone an injury, then you will surely find yourselves back again in jail to serve the rest of your sentences—plus a little extra."

"Ah! So you thinks we might meet up with someone we'd like to argue with, do you, Inspector?" Jenks pressed, his voice hard.

"I do. You have never troubled to conceal your hope for revenge, Jenks. To prevent you doing something which would result in Mark and Joe and Clifford being returned to jail, I have half a mind to arrest you now."

"Don't you worry, Inspector," snarled Riddell.

"No, just leave that to me," added Brennan. "Anyone

makes a break stopping me getting back will get a guts full of bash."

"So be it; d'you see that star?"

"That red star?" asked Myra. "Low down?"

"That's the one, Myra. It happens to be a light in a house window. That is the homestead called Mount Singular. Do you think you could walk there, now?"

"Now! I'll have a damn good try."

She rose to her feet without sign of fatigue, and the others were as agile.

"How far d'you reckon?" asked Brennan.

"About four miles. Hard miles, too, and a hard cliff at the end. I'd like to get there before midnight when most radio stations will be off the air. We'll walk single file. Mark, you take the rear. No talking. No striking matches."

Maddoch said, excitement shrilling his voice:

"We won't have to carry anything, will we?"

"Nothing," Riddell growled. "Only our ruddy selves."

Excitement sustained them over the first mile. Then Brennan fell, cursed wildly and lurched to his feet. The girl tripped and had to be assisted, and actually requested a halt and the flare of a match, that she could use her small mirror. The promontory on which Mount Singular was built eventually rose before them like a wall against the starry sky, and the 'star' which had beckoned them set like the moon behind a cloud.

As on that night in the long ago when they left the caverns, so now did they follow-my-leader, who had eyes with which to see, and a nose with which to scent. He led them in and out among the boulders and over the shallow gutters to the northern base of the promontory, and then, when bringing the bulk of land against the sky to determine the least difficult ascent, he stopped.

"Can you people smell what I smell?" he asked.

"Kerosene," replied the girl.

"Petrol," Brennan decided.

"A garage," voted Maddoch.

They appeared to be standing on a clear space, and Bony led them forward till stopped by an obstruction. They could just see his raised arms. They saw him stoop, and then heard him knock with a stone, on wood.

"Doors at the entrance to a cave," he said. "Wooden doors." He lay on the ground for a second or two. "Oil and petrol on the other side. Doors wide and high enough to admit a helicopter. Now for the final effort. And, for the last time, remember it rests with yourselves whether you go on to life and lights, or back to jail."

Chapter Twenty-Five

IT COULD HAVE BEEN WORSE

THE room was large, solidly furnished, serviced by two standard lamps. Against the wall opposite the french windows a stout redwood table supported the radio transceiver before which now sat Charles Weatherby.

His younger brother, Edgar, was wholly absorbed by an aviation journal. Nearer the french windows sat the wives of these two men; one sewing, the other idle, her glance fixed upon a picture her mind did not register. When the older woman spoke, she apparently didn't hear. Nor was she listening to her brother-in-law, who was saying:

"Yes, Jim. Two hundred fats. They ought to reach Kal on the 17th. I got permission to travel 'em through Lancefold, where there's plenty of feed at the back of the run. Will you see the boys through your place and on to town? Over."

A voice through the speaker said:

"O.K., Charles. I'll attend to that, and keep in touch with your men through Lancefold. That head stockman of yours in charge? Over."

"No," replied Weatherby. "Had to keep him back to muster a mob of stores to take down the line. Having missed that last rain here, our feed will dry off soon. How's things with you?"

The speaker said 'things' were reasonable. Weatherby was talking of feed prospects when the door was silently opened, and a figure appeared which brought his brother to his feet.

The figure looked like a wild aborigine wearing cast-off mission clothes for the first time in his life. Dark hair was over long, and the stubbly whiskers were matted. His feet were bare, and the trouser legs hung from the knees in shreds. This wild man ran across the room to stand beside the transceiver and point an automatic at the senior Weatherby.

"On your feet! Back! Farther back!" he ordered.

The large man obeyed. The wild man's eyes were hidden in the upper shadows cast by the lamp-shades, but the gun was clear enough.

"Who the hell are you? What the devil . . ."

"I am Detective-Inspector Bonaparte, alias William Black. There are five expendable cartridges in this weapon. Outside are friends of mine—gentlemen named Clifford Maddoch, Mark Brennan, Edward Jenks, and Joseph Riddell. A Mrs. Myra Thomas is with them. Also your head stockman. Being intelligent men, you will both realise that the situation has the element of danger, for you and your wives. Now contact Kalgoorlie."

"Be damned if we will," whispered the younger man, and took four paces forward. "You wouldn't shoot. You're a mighty big bluff. Inspector be damned!"

The french windows were rattled against their bolts, and one of the women cried out. The men spun about to see their head stockman flanked either side by reincarnations of the first bushrangers. Then the elder Weatherby turned again to Bony.

"They're all loose?" he asked, tightly.

"All but Doctor Havant. Why hesitate? They are dangerous men. Raise Kalgoorlie for me, at once."

"No!" shouted the other man. "We have guns, too."

"Dead men never aim straight," Bony reminded him, adding: "I always do."

"Charles!" called his wife. "Do what he says. He's right. Raise Kal."

The elder Weatherby slumped into the operator's chair and pushed down a switch and turned dials. Again the windows rattled against bolts. The women faced the threat from without. The younger man shrugged and withdrew to his chair, resignation in his dark eyes.

"Mount Singular calling! Come in Lancefold. Come in Kalgoorlie. Mount Singular calling. Urgently calling Kalgoorlie. Over."

He switched over, and a voice deeply resonant spoke.

"Kalgoorlie Base, Mount Singular. I am getting you clearly."

"Inspector Bonaparte speaking from Mount Singular, Kalgoorlie. Hold it a moment. Mrs. Weatherby! Admit those persons before they break through. Just another moment, Kalgoorlie."

Those outside surged into the room, pushing the head stockman before them. Bony signalled silence with his hand, palm outward. "Brennan, come here. You others remain inactive for one minute. Now, Mark, watch these Weatherbys while I report to Kalgoorlie. Take a message, Kalgoorlie. Over."

Bony motioned to the elder Weatherby, and then the speaker announced that Kalgoorlie was ready, adding:

"We have been alerted for you to contact us, Inspector."

Weatherby worked on switch and dials, and Bony replied:

"Thank you, Kalgoorlie. A message for Superintendent Wyeth—per phone. Inspector Bonaparte reports he is at Mount Singular, together with Mrs. Myra Thomas, and the following men who failed the conditions of their parole:

Mark Brennan, Joseph Riddell, Clifford Maddoch and Edward Jenks. Despite extreme provocation, these men are behaving with commendable restraint, but the situation could be explosive and I need assistance with all speed. Got that, Kalgoorlie? Over."

"Every word, Inspector. Keep on the air."

Silence, and during the silence reaction hit them hard. Bony's hopes to skate over this emotional ice were frustrated by Maddoch who pointed to the junior Weatherby and shouted:

"I know you. You're the man I met on the train going to my brother's place, the man who coshed me on the station platform. You're the man who kidnapped me. You vile creature!"

"He! He!" sniggered Jenks from somewhere amid whiskers like a circular chimney broom. He mimicked "Vile creature! So now we know where we are, and now we know why you keep that helicopter in the cave at the foot of the cliff outside. I been waitin' a long long time for this."

"Jenks!" Bony said sharply.

Jenks remained tense, ready to go into action. He glared at Bony, downward to the automatic. Riddell spoke up:

"Caw! Stop the how-doin' and get us some grub and a bottle or two of whisky. Plenty of time to argue."

"Of course there is," supported the girl. "We're not standing for any rough-house, Jenks. Not now when the bright lights are only just round the corner. Smashing up these people and this place won't get us anywhere but back to jail. Be your age, idiot."

"Gimme the gun, Inspector," pleaded Brennan. "You're too much of a gent to handle this. I'll stop Ted while you are thinkin' about doing something. No more ruddy jail for me. I've had a bit more'n I can take."

"You guard that transceiver, Mark," Bony ordered. "Ladies! Food, and coffee or tea. Please. Here."

The older woman nodded and made for the door. Myra Thomas lurched after her, crying:

"I want a bath, and clean clothes. I want . . ."

The speaker said, stentorianly:

"Superintendent Wyeth calling Inspector Bonaparte. Over to you, Mount Singular."

Bony stepped backward towards the receiver, had to turn to the elder Weatherby for a second, and this gave Jenks his chance. The ex-sailor leaped for Edgar Weatherby, evading Riddell's grasp. Then Jenks had his hands about the throat of the seated Edgar, and was pressing him down into the back of the chair. The speaker continued to announce that Superintendent Wyeth was calling Inspector Bonaparte. Credit must be given to Riddell for acting promptly, but he was slower than the aborigine head stockman, who, sweeping up another chair, brought the front edge of the seat down upon Jenks's cannon-ball head.

This outraged loyalties. Brennan jumped past Bony and waded in with Riddell, to subdue the head stockman. Maddoch hovered on the outskirts. He grabbed another chair, then collapsed on the floor, turned on his chest, and began to cry with rage. The younger Mrs. Weatherby screamed and ran from the room. Her husband was nursing his lacerated throat, and Superintendent Wyeth still called for Inspector Bonaparte. Because of the poor physical condition of the white men, there was considerable damage done to the room's furnishings before the black man was finally put to sleep.

"Over to Mount Singular," ordered Bony. "Right! Inspector Bonaparte calling, Superintendent. I was delayed in answering your call by a slight diversion. Send relief as quickly as it can be managed. Please note. The persons

listed in my first message were incarcerated by these
Weatherbys, in underground caverns on the northern
extremity of the Plain. Motive—out of this world, but
acceptable. I am happy to report that they have behaved
well and are continuing to do so. They deserve every
consideration. Over."

"Quite a tale, Bonaparte. Quite a tale. There's a man
named Fiddler, another named Mitski, and Doctor Havant.
Do they enter into it? Over."

"Yes. Fiddler and Mitski are dead. Havant we left in the
caverns as he wasn't fit to tramp two hundred miles over the
Plain."

"Big thing, Bonaparte. Organised conspiracy?"

"Well organised. It would be wise to keep all this from
the Press until you choose to release it. Security doesn't
count. It's all ours. Over."

"Good! Well, the man at Rawlinna is on his way, and
Easter is being contacted to leave at once. I'll charter a
plane and the pilot will arrange to arrive out there when it's
light enough to see a landing. Tell those people with you
that your report on them will be noted, and they'll have
nothing to worry about. Perth is waiting for me. Stay on
the air."

Brennan smiled into Bony's cold blue eyes.

"Thanks for making it a bit sweet for us, Inspector."

"We have several hours ahead of us, Mark. Is Jenks
dead? And that aborigine?"

"The abo could be. No chair ever made could kill Jenks.
What a man!"

"Joe! Where is Riddell?"

"Gone looking for grub, I think. Couldn't wait."

"Call him."

Brennan went to the door and shouted. Riddell came in.
He was chewing on a leg of mutton. Bony sighed.

"Joe, sit there and eat, and watch these two men. Mark, hunt for something to tie Jenks up with, and make it snappy. I'll have to look-see Clifford. He seems to be all in."

With thankfulness he was careful not to betray, Bony sat at ease eating sandwiches and sipping hot coffee. He was feeling that at last he was indeed master of the situation, and that he had strategically placed all these people to await the hour help arrived.

Maddoch slept in utter exhaustion on the settee. Riddell was still gnawing into his leg of mutton. Brennan was the life of the party. He was feeding sandwiches to Jenks who sat on the floor, his arms lashed to his sides and his feet tied, and with his back to the wall. The head stockman was just tied hands and feet. He continued to dwell in another place. The two women and their husbands sat and glowered. Only Myra Thomas was absent. Presently the younger Mrs. Weatherby rose and dragged her chair, to sit almost knee to knee before Bony. Her husband attempted to rise, waved his hands in resignation, and absently loaded a pipe.

Mrs. Weatherby's dark eyes searched Bony's face.

"Did I hear you say that Igor Mitski is dead, Inspector?"

"Yes. He was killed by a falling rock, Mrs. Weatherby."

"I'm very glad, Inspector. You know, of course, that he murdered my little girl?" Bony nodded. "He hit her with his fist. Then he picked her up by the feet and swung her round and dashed her head against the door-post. Do you approve of that kind of thing?"

"I do not, Mrs. Weatherby. But I think you are wrong on the details. Isn't that so, Mark?"

"Not much, Inspector. The lady's always right an' all that."

"Not then quite as you related it, Brennan."

"That is what he did to my little Mayflower, Inspector," the woman continued, her voice soft, but her eyes hardening, and her slim nostrils beginning to flare. Her sister pleaded:

"Jean! You had better come away from the Inspector. He'll let us go and lie down till this is all over. Please, Inspector."

"Yes, do," Bony agreed. Abruptly, Mrs. Edgar Weatherby stood, and words built into shrilled sentences as the emotional dam broke.

"No!" she shouted. "No, I stay. It was my idea in the beginning and I take all the responsibility. I am the mother of the murdered. I persuaded my husband to join me in executing justice. I organised all those others who sought justice for their murdered. Now listen, all of you, because after tonight I shall never open my mouth again about this matter; my husband won't, and my sister and her husband won't."

Bony witnessed the effort to regain control, the facial muscles working, the mouth firming above the square chin of this now dominant woman.

"It's like carrying coals to Newcastle, Inspector, to tell you what has been going on in this country, and especially in those States long controlled by the lower orders. We all know that in Australia there is a growing section of the people who are indifferent to crime, and a certain section who are definitely sympathetic towards murderers. Proof! When that Thomas woman was acquitted, she was greeted outside the court by a huge crowd of cheering people.

"Our aim is for justice on behalf of the murdered. We have to accept the verdict pronounced by a judge in court, but justice is stamped in the mud when a gang of politicians flout the sentence of the judge and release the murderer years before he has served his sentence; flouting justice to make themselves popular.

"They pander to men and women who have the lust to murder in their hearts, but lack the courage to strike. They pander to people who resent laws, hate the police, hate any restraint placed on their vile emotions.

"Hanging was too drastic for the murderer of my little girl; too cruel for the murderer of that young bridal couple; too heathenish for the killer of the farmer who objected to his animals being ill-treated; unthinkable for the wife slayer; too unkind for the abortionist! Twelve years they gave the murderer of my child. Then the vote catchers stepped in and freed him after eleven years. Mark Brennan—never to be released, but he was. Maddoch and the others, released years before they served the sentence imposed by a competent judge. Yesterday—death. Today—a few years in prison. Tomorrow—a few months' detention."

"Today—a Fellowship," drawled Mark Brennan.

Mrs. Weatherby turned to stare at Brennan. She frowned, wiped him off like a gnat.

"The world has fallen into decay, its standards are rotten because it's ruled by men crazed by power," she went on. "My man, my men relatives, sit back and moan and do nothing. So I had to, Inspector. I simply had to obey the voices and give peace to the murdered. I'm not naming my assistants; you will never find proof. We found helpers even in the Departments of Justice who told us when a murderer was to be released. So we were able to waylay him and take him to those caverns. That is all I have to say. It is all I shall ever say."

The room became silent. The woman with the square chin and haunted eyes continued to face Bony, who looked at this moment like Ned Kelly himself. Bony said:

"How long did you intend keeping the men in those caverns?"

"Till they died."

As she rose and was about to turn to her sister, there stepped into the room a young lady superbly arrayed in white linen.

"Now I am ready to eat," Myra Thomas announced.

The Weatherby women passed her on their way to the door. To them Myra Thomas was something unmentionable.

Chapter Twenty-Six

REALLY MERITED

JENKS exclaimed:

"Caw! Look at Lady Myra Muckhead!"

"Seems I've missed something," the girl said, speaking to Bony. "Ask someone to bring me something to eat and drink. I'm starving."

"Plenty of eats in the kitchen," rumbled Riddell. "Ruddy well go and stuff out there, Myra. Gents only in here."

"Is that transceiver open to Kalgoorlie?" she asked Bony, and he nodded. "Has the Press come through?"

"No. Go and find yourself supper. I'd like more coffee, too."

"What a nerve, Inspector! I'm not a servant." The almost purple eyes glowed with anger, but the carefully creamed and powdered face was restrained from showing emotion.

"Bring more coffee all round, Myra," he said. "We have a long wait before us. You might make sure that those two ladies have retired to their rooms. Try to be helpful for once."

"And bring a snifter for this nig," Jenks ordered. "He's coming out of dreamland. Lazy old coot." The aborigine groaned, and Jenks said: "Hey, Inspector! What about takin' these ropes off me? I'll be quiet. Give you me word."

The girl brought the coffee. Bony assisted the head

stockman to sit up and take notice of it. He made a cigarette for Jenks, saying that if he dropped it from his mouth he could retrieve it from the floor with his mouth. From thence onward, he and they sat and waited.

Riddell and Brennan were asleep, the elder Weatherby appeared to be asleep, the girl was engrossed by magazines when the speaker said:

"Superintendent Wyeth is leaving now, Inspector Bonaparte, and will land at daybreak. I am to say that you can expect Constable Easter at around four o'clock, and Sergeant Lush from Rawlinna an hour later. Over."

"Thank you, Kalgoorlie. All quiet here."

It was twenty minutes to four when they heard the jeep, and a few moments later Constable Easter entered by the french windows. Bony rose to meet him, and Easter took five seconds to recognise him.

"Constable Easter!" exclaimed Myra Thomas. "How nice to meet you. I'm Myra Thomas. Could I bring you some coffee and a sandwich?"

Easter was rocked, but he took it like a real man.

"I'd be glad if you would, Mrs. Thomas." He surveyed the others, pondered on the recumbent forms of the aborigine and Jenks, looked into Bony's eyes for a full second, and sat down. "I know only that you had arrived here, Inspector, and needed assistance."

Bony related his adventures following their parting outside the wicket fence. He introduced with grave politeness those he had brought from the caverns, and sketched the story Mrs. Edgar Weatherby had given them. Easter was further rocked, and took it like a real policeman. Bony could have been telling a fairy tale.

"Before we took over here, Easter," he went on, "we found with no difficulty an open cave where the helicopter is kept, then we intruded on the head stockman and brought him in with us. How Mr. Weatherby obtained the machine, and how he brought it here unobserved, can be cleared up later. Possibly he was a pilot during the war. Two other matters we can clear up now, or when you have eaten something. As Sergeant Lush will arrive soon, perhaps you would like to eat whilst we clear these up."

"An idea, Inspector. I'm ready."

"Riddell! Brennan! Get the aborigine to his feet." The stockman was hauled up. He needed repairs and was badly frightened. "You are a medicine man," Bony stated, and the whites of the black eyes expanded. "When I left with the camels, you were told to track me? Tell me the truth. You need not be afraid . . . afterwards. How far did you track me?"

"Out to bore. Sammy Pickup, he was riding after steers and he saw the camels out on the Plain. He tell Boss."

"The Boss told you sit-down and make talk with medicine man up north?"

"Yair. That's right. Boss said for me to make talk with Luritja man. I sit down. I make talk, and make talk, and bimeby I know Luritja man he hear and make talk to me."

"What did the Boss tell you to make talk about?"

The medicine man glanced at the Weatherbys, but the elder could still be asleep and the younger brother stared at his shoes.

"So you gather little sticks and rub magic into them with your churinga stone," Bony pressed, and the aborigine's face brightened, and he nodded. "You make fire with little sticks, and you sit-down before the fire, and presently your spirit leaves you to fly through the air to meet the spirit of the Luritja man. What did you tell to him?"

"I tell him Boss says to tell him you are making for desert, looking for Patsy Lonergan's traps. Boss say for me to tell

Luritja man to hang round, and if you find where white men are hid he's to put you with 'em, and everything you have, but not rifle and pack ropes. Luritja says, 'all right.' He says next time fly-machine goes, for to leave plenty bacco and rations at same place. So I tell Boss,.and Boss says, 'good-oh'."

"All right," Bony told him. "You can go. Untie him."

Myra Thomas gripped his arm, saying:

"Is that dinkum? It is all true, that way of talking?"

"Dinkum for me, Myra," he said.

"But what a story! What a script that will make!" Turning, she almost ran to the elder Weatherby, shaking him saying:

"Paper. Writing paper, quick. And a pencil."

"Was I right?" asked Easter, and Bony smiled affirm-matively.

"Now we come to Edward Jenks," Bony said. "Stand him up, please." Brennan and Riddell supported him. Maddoch came, and the girl with a pad and pencil. "Constable Easter will arrest you, Edward Jenks, on the charge of having murdered Igor Mitski. I shall do my duty by doing all possible to make that charge stick.

"Riddell has said that he thought he saw Maddoch strike Mitski, but the situation of the wound was such that Maddoch's height relative to that of the victim absolves him. Although not as tall as Mitski you are not much taller than Maddoch, hence Riddell's mistake. Unlike Maddoch, you are athletic. You are capable of jumping high, as all of us have so often observed. It was when at the apex of a jump that you smashed the rock against Mitski's head, for that jump placed you at the same height as your victim."

"You won't make that stick, Inspector," sneered the grinning Jenks."

"Before you killed Mitski, Jenks, in your mind was

213

the picture of the hen in a yard with many roosters, and you planned to eliminate all your rivals. That plan became less attractive on recognising me."

"You got no witnesses, for a start," Jenks claimed. Into the sweep of his eyes he took the three released murderers, and Bony saw them nod assent.

"You could be mistaken, Jenks," he said, coldly. "Such is my reputation, when you discovered me with you you felt you must do something about the rock. Your opportunity came only when I asked for additional lamps, and you went to the kitchen for those lamps. You tossed the rock on to Myra's bed to implicate her. Why? Because she baited you."

"You mongrel!" spat Myra Thomas. "I'll witness against you. And you others will, too . . . or else."

Jenks was formally arrested and cautioned by Easter, and a little later, Riddell drew Bony aside to say:

"We're out of it now, Inspector. What happened in them caverns don't count no longer. I'm sort of sorry . . ."

"I believe I understand, Riddell. Loyalty among thieves, no. Loyalty among killers could be firm. I could break that down, but I am now telling you something you don't know. Jenks tried to implicate Myra by tossing on to her bed the rock with which he killed Mitski, and that doesn't call for loyalty. I could have all of you held on suspicion of complicity."

Riddell shrugged, and Maddoch said:

"You could, Inspector, but you won't. We played the game, and you will. You wouldn't take it out on us."

"What wouldn't he take out on us?" interrupted Brennan, and Maddoch explained. "Not you, Inspector. Only an hour back, when Jenks was threatening to break out, I told you you're too much of a gent. You'll do your job. You'll go your hardest. But you won't go that hard to shove us all in back again. D'you know what?"

"What, Mark?" asked the smiling Bonaparte.

"We were all right before that bitch was dumped down among us. We never made her a member, you know. Had to draw the line somewhere." Without, was born a sound as of a top, and the sound swiftly became a low roar. "More flatfoots arriving. The place will be chocker with 'em in a minute. Will you keep in touch, Inspector, afterwards?"

"Yes. Why not?"

"Cheers! When we get old Doc Havant back, the Institute will have to have an annual get-together. Will you come?"

"Well, I suppose that will be a duty, being a Fellow," agreed Bony.

He took from a pocket the small rock slab on which Brennan had engraved the Fellowship, and Easter came and looked over his shoulder and wanted to know what the letters meant. Slowly, Bony recited:

"Fellow of the Released Murderers' Institute. I really earned that, Easter."

ARTHUR W. UPFIELD

WINDS OF EVIL

When Detective-Inspector Napoleon Bonaparte sets out to investigate two bizarre murders at Wirragatta Station all the odds are against him. The crimes were committed a year before and the scent is now cold, and any clues that have survived have been confused by a bumbling policeman.

As Bony follows the trail, he is first threatened and then attacked by the mysterious murderer. It's a case which taxes his ingenuity to the limit.

DEATH OF A SWAGMAN

"Our distinctive student of violence arrives incognito at Merino, in western New South Wales, and, as a first move, provokes the local sergeant to lock him up. The method in Bony's madness is that while serving a semi-detention sentence and being made to paint the police station, he wears the best of all disguises . . . Here again is a first-rate Upfield mystery, made warm by humour, by the background characters and his portrayal of the natural background scene."

— The Age, Melbourne.

ORDER MORE BOOKS IN THIS SERIES DIRECT FROM THE PUBLISHER

Titles available in this series include:

The Sands of Windee

Winds of Evil

Mr Jelly's Business

The Bone is Pointed

Bushranger of the Skies

Death of a Swagman

The Devil's Steps

An Author Bites the Dust

The Widows of Broome

Man of Two Tribes

The Battling Prophet

Please send me the following Upfield novels at a cost of $2.95 each plus 80c post and packaging per title.

Titles requested: ....
....
....

Name: ....

Address: ....
.... Postcode: ....

Payment by cheque ☐ money order ☐ Bankcard ☐

Bankcard number ....

Expiry Date ....

Signature ....